FROM SUNSET TILL SUNRISE

SUNSET TILL SUNRISE

JONATHAN ROSEN

Sky Pony Press
New York

First Edition

This is a work of fiction. Names, characters, places, and incidents are from the author's imagination and are used fictitiously.

Sky Pony Press books may be purchased in bulk at special discounts for sales promotion, corporate gifts, fund-raising, or educational purposes. Special editions can also be created to specifications. For details, contact the Special Sales Department, Sky Pony Press, 307 West 36th Street, 11th Floor, New York, NY 10018 or info@skyhorsepublishing.com.

Sky Pony® is a registered trademark of Skyhorse Publishing, Inc.®, a Delaware corporation.

Visit our website at www.skyponypress.com.

10 9 8 7 6 5 4 3 2 1

Library of Congress Cataloging-in-Publication Data is available on file.

Cover design by Kate Gardner
Cover illustration by Xavier Bonet

Print ISBN: 978-1-5107-3409-8
Ebook ISBN: 978-1-5107-3410-4

Printed in the United States of America

This book is dedicated to my family: Michele, Shaylee, David, Maya, and Parker. Without the sacrifices all of you make, none of this would be possible.

CHAPTER ONE

THERE'S SOMETHING ABOUT LILY

A general rule of thumb is that vampires make bad neighbors. It's not a hard and fast rule, but it's one that you have to at least be aware of. Not that I'm even sure that mine are really vampires, but there's at least some suspicion. Mostly from my cousin Tommy.

It's tough to argue with him about it since he seems to have a knack for sniffing these things out.

You see, Tommy is something of a conspiracy theorist when it comes to the supernatural.

To be fair, he's probably studied this stuff more than any twelve-year-old ever should. Not that I can blame him. Because, for one, we live in the town of Gravesend, where pretty much anywhere you turn you run into some sort of weird or creepy thing happening. And two, it's entirely possible that there's already

1

been some circumstantial evidence that my across-the-street neighbors might be a little more than they seem. Mainly the fact that they've lived there for four months already, and not once have I ever seen them during the day. A fact that Tommy reminds me of every chance he gets.

There's also the fact that we did see movers bringing a coffin into the house. Even though they said it was a prop from some movie, and that the owner was a collector or actor or something, it still set off a few alarm bells.

The worst part about all of this? Tommy. It was bad enough that he thought he knew everything. If he was right about this, there'd be no living with him.

And it didn't help matters that only a few months earlier he had been right about a mob of marauding stuffed animals coming to life, but that's another story.

So, I guess right now he feels he like should get a little benefit of the doubt. And he probably should, but I mean, seriously, vampires are *so* last century.

Anyway, to be completely honest, there was also one other reason why I brushed all talk of vampires aside.

A girl.

Problem was, I didn't even know her name.

The only things I could tell you were she was around my age, maybe a little taller than me, and had long, dark hair. I also imagined her to have a bright smile and, for some reason, a great laugh, but I really couldn't tell you for sure, because we'd never even said one word to each other. But there was just something different about her. Something that drew me to her.

Still, it would've been nice to know *something*. I didn't even know what school she went to. All I knew was that it wasn't mine and that for the last several months, ever since she moved in across the street, I did just about anything to be outside at the same time that she was. Every night after school I would peek through my window, and if she took out the trash, so would I. If she went out to her yard for something, I'd go for a walk. Anything, really, just to get a chance to see her.

Talking though, that was another matter.

I think there might have been a momentary meeting of the eyes once, but I couldn't swear to it.

I kept hoping that the next time would be the time we'd speak. So far, I'd done this routine night after night and week after week for the past few months. She usually came out at the same time, right after dinner, and it was great. Well, except for the speaking part. Unfortunately, there were other times when a monkey wrench got thrown into my plans.

And that wrench happened to be eight years old and the number-one source of aggravation in my life.

My sister Abby.

"Mom! Devin's spying on the neighbor again!"

3

Even though Abby was four years younger, somehow she was the one who would usually torment me. I had to admit, though, she did a very good job of it.

"I'm not spying!" I knew it sounded hollow.

Mom walked into the room. "Abby, leave him alone." She turned to me and smiled. "The girl across the street?"

I just about wanted to die right there, but tried to play it off. "What girl across the street?"

Abby's brow furrowed. "You can stop pretending. Everybody knows you like her."

I glared at her. "Everybody knows you're annoying too, but it doesn't stop you from doing it."

Abby stomped her foot. "Mom!"

"Devin!"

"Dad!" I pleaded, but from the sounds of his snores coming from the couch, I knew he'd be no help. I sighed. "I don't even know who you're talking about."

"Yeah, right." Abby thrust her arm toward the window. "Look, there she is!"

I whipped my head around, but the only thing there was the first glimpse of the moon appearing in the sky.

Abby laughed. "See? You're not fooling anyone."

That right there is everything you need to know about Abby.

Mom walked over to the window and peered out. "Well, I think it's cute." She craned her neck to look some more. "I don't think I've ever really seen her too much. Maybe I'll invite her family over for dinner."

I threw my hands out in front of me. "No! No dinner. Remember what happened the last time you invited a neighbor to dinner?"

She turned back to us. "Yes, we made a nice friend, and Herb gets the two of you toys from his company all the time."

"When they don't try to kill us," I said.

Mom frowned. "Devin, that's enough. Anyway, we're going to eat dinner soon, and I don't want either of you up late. We're all going to the mall early tomorrow."

I rolled my eyes. "The *mall*? I don't want to go to the mall. It's spring break. I want to relax."

"There'll be plenty of time to play this week. I want to get there early and get a nice family picture with the Easter Bunny."

I felt my breath leave me. "Please, no bunnies."

Mom shot me a look. "Devin, there's no reason to be scared of bunnies anymore."

"I'm not scared, but I'm too old to take pictures with the Easter Bunny."

Abby gasped. "*We're not going to see the Easter Bunny tomorrow?*" She stomped her foot. "But I want to see the Easter Bunny!"

Mom's nostrils flared. She glanced at Abby, and then looked back at me. She gritted her teeth. "It's going to be Easter soon, and we're going to take a family picture with the bunny!"

I recognized that tone well. It meant that no matter what I said or what points I made, we were going to take a picture with the Easter Bunny tomorrow morning.

The doorbell rang.

"Who's that?" I asked.

"I told you that Tommy's coming to sleep over for a few nights."

I had totally forgotten that he was staying with us while his parents were going on a seven-day cruise. They were calling it their "second honeymoon." For some reason, they didn't want to bring him along.

All I knew was that it meant having to be stuck with him for a week.

Mom headed for the door, and Abby trailed after her.

I waited a second until they left and then ran to the window. My shoulders sagged. Still no sign of her.

"You're looking in the wrong spot," said a voice from behind me.

I turned to see Tommy walking in, carrying a backpack.

"What are you talking about?" I asked.

He hitched his thumb over his shoulder. "Your girl-friend isn't across the street."

I winced. "Shhhh!" I glanced at the couch, but Dad was still snoring away. I waited a second to be sure he was still sleeping and turned back to Tommy. "Will you stop saying that? Abby is already making me miserable about it, and now my mom is starting too. I don't want them talking about her."

He snorted. "Well, it's too late for that."

My heart dropped. "What do you mean?"

He pointed toward the door. "It means that right this very second, your mom and Abby are out in front of your house, talking to your girlfriend."

A fog came over me, like his words slowed and echoed throughout the room. Mom and Abby . . . talking to her . . . *before me?* "You're lying, and she's not my girlfriend."

Tommy shook his head. "Relax, I don't actually think she's your girlfriend. It's probably not even possible with her being a vampire and all. Dating would be difficult, unless you only see her at night."

"Stop it. She's not a vampire."

"They had a coffin. They're vampires," Tommy said.

"The movers said they collected movie memorabilia. I bet he's an actor."

He arched an eyebrow. "Then why have we never seen him?"

I shrugged. "I don't know, maybe he's just shy. It doesn't mean he's a vampire."

Tommy shot me a look, like he didn't believe me. "A shy actor? No way. They all love the spotlight. And besides, we've gone near her house a ton of times already and have never seen him. And that's not even talking about her."

"What about her?"

"You've still never seen her during the day?"

I thought a moment and frowned. "No, but we have school."

Tommy shook his head. "On weekends there's no school, and we never see her during the day then." He paused a moment. His eyes widened. "Wait a second. I got it." He pounded his fist into his hand. "It's possible that she's his human caretaker or eternal slave, forced to guard the vampire while he sleeps." He ran his fingers through his hair. "This is way worse than I thought."

I sighed. "Okay, seriously, you've been watching way too many movies."

"Whatever you say. But when you wake up dead one night, drained of all your blood, you'll wish you had listened to me."

"How would I wake up dead? That's doesn't even make any sense. It's impossible."

He rolled his eyes. "It's not impossible, because you'd be undead. Dead . . . but un."

"You're a moron."

"Yeah, would a moron bring this?" He ripped open his backpack.

The smell hit me right away. I waved my hand in front of my nose. "Is that—"

He nodded. "Yep! Garlic. Don't worry, I brought enough for both of us."

I coughed, and my eyes teared up. "You brought enough for an army. Now put that away before you stink up the whole house." I took a peek at the front door. "I'm going out to see what's going on."

"I'll go with you."

"Okay." I pointed to the backpack. "But leave that here."

He frowned and shoved everything back in. "Fine."

We marched across the room and opened the door.

I stopped in my tracks. There were certain moments in life where no words could do justice to the images you saw. This was one of them.

Standing in front of the house was Mom, with Abby by her side. And just like Tommy said, they were talking to the girl from across the street.

My heart thumped.

They all turned toward us.

I opened my mouth but no words came out.

"Oh, there they are," Mom said.

The girl looked at me. Her eyes sparkled.

Everything inside me felt like it was twisting into knots.

Mom pointed to us. "That's Devin and my nephew,

9

Tommy." She put her hand on the girl's back. "And this is our neighbor, Lily."

Lily waved. "Hi."

I lifted my hand partway. "Hi." It squeaked out.

Abby peered out from behind Mom and smirked.

"Devin," Mom said. "Lily is here about an event at her school." She turned to Lily. "Do you want to tell him about it?"

She smiled and her whole face lit up. "I was just telling your mom that this Friday night my school is having a dance to try to get new students. It's going to be really great. You should come."

"Your school?" I asked.

Mom interrupted. "Yes, Lily goes to a private school in the area. That's why you don't see her in yours."

I winced. Just great. Now Lily knew we'd been discussing her. *Thanks, Mom.*

If Lily realized it, she didn't let on. "We're supposed to bring as many people as we can, and since I've seen you around the neighborhood, I thought maybe you might like to go?"

"Devin would *looooooove* to go," Abby sang.

I gritted my teeth and glared at her.

Mom swatted Abby lightly on her head. "Quiet."

"Ow!" Abby yelled.

"What school do you go to?" I asked.

"Nosfer Academy," Lily said.

I blinked. "I never heard of it."

Lily shrugged. "Well, the whole name is Nosfer Academy of Talented Understudies." She laughed. "We're all understudies until we graduate. Then we become trained actors. It's a performing arts school."

"Did you say actor?" I glanced at Tommy.

He frowned.

Mom clasped her hands together. "Oh, I love theater! I used to perform in high school. I played the part of third munchkin in our senior production of *The Wizard of Oz!*" She turned to me. "I wish Devin would show an interest in acting."

Lily smiled. "Well, maybe after he sees the school he'll want to transfer and become one of us." She pointed. "And your cousin can come to the dance too."

Tommy took a step behind me. "I'll go get the garlic," he whispered.

I elbowed him in the chest.

"So, what do you say?" Mom asked. "Do you want to go?"

I took a peek at Mom and turned back to Lily. This was the closest I'd ever been to her, and she was even prettier than I thought. There was just something about her.

"Uh . . ." *Oh no!* The words were stuck in my throat!

Abby giggled. "He wants to go."

Mom swatted her again.

"Ow!" Abby rubbed her head.

Thankfully, Mom cut in. "We'll discuss it, and he'll let you know tomorrow, okay?"

"Absolutely." She turned and looked back across the street. "Well, I'd better get going. My dad's probably waiting for me to come back so we can go for dinner."

Mom arched an eyebrow. "Oh? It's just you and your dad?"

Lily looked away. She wiped at her eye. "Yeah, my mom's no longer with us."

Mom's bottom lip pushed out. "I'm so sorry to hear that."

Lily nodded slowly. "Thank you. It happened a long time ago. She had a rare blood disorder. I don't like to talk about it."

Tommy cleared his throat. I ignored him.

"Well," Mom said. "You tell your dad that we'd love to have you over for dinner sometime."

Lily's face brightened. "Really? Is that an invitation?"

Tommy gulped behind me.

Mom nodded. "Yes, it is. Anytime."

Lily eyed me for a moment, and smiled again "That's great, thank you. You don't know how happy that'll make him. We always go out to eat or order in; it'll be nice to have something home-cooked for once." She turned to me. "It was nice meeting you, Devin and Tommy."

I opened my mouth, but still nothing.

She waved and ran across the street to her house.

Tommy put his hand on my shoulder, leaned in, and whispered, "I told you before, and you didn't believe me. You have a vampire problem."

CHAPTER TWO

THE VR FILE

There are times in everyone's life when they make choices that they'll later regret. Discussing Lily—and the dance she invited me to—with Tommy was sure to be one of mine.

The rain pelted against my window and streaks of lightning flashed.

Tommy paced back and forth across my room. "Okay, the way I see it, you have to turn down Lily's invitation and hole up in your house for a little while. Not long, maybe only twenty or thirty years, until the next generation of kids is older."

"Why would I turn down her invitation? I've wanted to talk to her ever since she moved in. And then she invites me to a dance? Yeah, good idea to turn her down."

Tommy shook his head slowly. "Oh, Devin, Devin, Devin. Poor, naïve Devin."

"What are you talking about now?"

He sighed. "Did you ever stop to think why the girl that you've been liking, but never spoken to, suddenly, out of the blue, comes over and invites you to a dance?"

I shrugged. "I don't know, maybe she's being nice."

He waved me off. "Nobody's *that* nice."

I hated when he got like this. Always acting like he knew more than I did. "She's new in the neighborhood. Maybe this is her way of reaching out to make friends?"

"Just suddenly? All these months she's been here and *now* she's asking you?" He shook his head. "I don't buy it."

"You don't have to buy it. And besides, did *you* ever stop to think that just maybe she liked me too?"

Tommy snorted. "Oh, please. She's so out of your league. No offense."

"Yeah, why would I be offended at that?" I stared out the window into the night. With the wind and downpour, it was hard to make out anything. The shadows were playing tricks on me. It seemed like there was something moving in the trees. I leaned closer to the window until my forehead was pressing against the glass.

Tommy stood next to me and peered out. "What are you staring at?"

"I don't know. I thought I saw something out there."

"A bat?"

"Stop it. There's no such thing as vampires," I said, more for my benefit than for his.

"Like there was no such thing as warlocks or magical stuffed animals. I've told you before, Gravesend is a different place. Lots of weird things happen here."

I tapped the glass. "There's no way that girl's a vampire. She was so pretty and sweet."

He laughed. "That's how they lure you in. Didn't you ever watch any vampire movies?"

"Yeah, so?"

He tapped the side of his head. "Think about it! Have you ever seen an ugly vampire?"

I shrugged. "I don't know. I never really thought about it."

"You don't have to. The answer is *no*. There are no ugly vampires. They're all good-looking."

"I'm sure that's not true. There have got to be *some* ugly vampires."

"Nope, not one. And that's how they attract the plain and ugly-looking people. No offense."

"I want you to know your 'no offense' comments are really offensive."

He rolled his eyes. "Don't be so sensitive. All I'm saying is, on your own, a girl like that would never go for you."

I turned away from him and stared out the window again. The rain hit like handfuls of gravel striking the glass. "You know, every time I talk to you I come away feeling worse about myself."

"And I've never heard anyone whine as much as you do. I'm trying to save your life here." He placed his hand on my shoulder. "Now, where do you stand on wooden stakes?"

I swatted his hand away. "Who has wooden stakes? And she's not a vampire!"

"Okay, let's agree to disagree about that. But just for argument's sake, let's just say that she is. Wouldn't it be better if you're prepared?"

A pain shot through my head, like an icepick jamming into my eye. The usual onset of my Tommy headache. "What are you saying? More holy water?"

He snapped his fingers. "Yes! Good idea. I'll have to get to Father Merrin again. I think he's having a special this week."

"A special on holy water? Why would *anyone* need so much holy water?"

He held his hand up. "I don't ask questions. There are some things that we're better off not knowing. Trust me."

"You're a moron."

"Again, we'll agree to disagree about that." He started pacing. "Now. Let's see what else we need. Wait! I got it. Silver. We also need silver."

"That's for werewolves."

"It's for vampires too," Tommy insisted.

"I don't think you know what you're talking about."

"Who's the expert here?"

"There's no right answer to that."

He walked over to my dresser and started searching through everything. "Do you have anything to write with? I don't want us to forget anything."

"You only said two things so far."

"Yeah, two *important* things." He searched a little more before finally stopping. "Here we go!" He held up a notebook and pen.

"That's my history notebook."

"So? Just call this the history of vampires. You'll get another one for school." He tapped it. "From now on, this is for vampire research." He scrawled something across the front. "We'll call it the VR File, so nobody else will understand what we're talking about."

"*I* don't understand what you're talking about."

Again, he ignored me, then tossed me the notebook and pen. He snapped his fingers. "Well?"

"Well, what?"

"Do I have to tell you everything? *Start taking notes.*"

I have no idea why I listened to him, but it was usually my first instinct. I opened the notebook and started writing.

He continued to pace, walking slowly, while rubbing his chin. "Okay, we have silver, wooden stakes, garlic. Actually, put down lots of garlic." He jabbed his finger in the air. "Crosses! We can't forget crosses."

"I wouldn't dream of it."

"There's fire, and, oh!" He snapped his fingers again. "Beheading. If you take off a vampire's head, it kills them."

"Taking off *anyone's* head would kill them."

"Are you going to make sarcastic comments every time I say something, or take this seriously?"

I tossed the notebook onto my bed. "This is ridiculous. She's not a vampire."

He paused, turned away from me, and looked out the window. "Did I ever tell you the story of Billy Thompson?"

I groaned. "Oh, no . . ."

"Billy Thompson was a kid around our age who lived in Gravesend, close to thirty years ago."

"You're making this up."

He ignored me and kept going. "One day, Billy's parents invited what they thought was a new neighbor into their house."

"What kind of a name is Billy Thompson? That's the best you could do? It doesn't even sound real."

He exhaled loudly. "Will you stop interrupting? I'm going to lose my train of thought." He remained silent a moment. "Now where was I?"

I sighed. "Billy Thompson's neighbor."

"Right. Anyway, this neighbor had a daughter, and Billy quickly realized that *she* was a vampire, but the problem was nobody believed him."

"Is there a point to this?"

Tommy held his index finger to his lips. "*Shhh!*" He continued talking to me but stared out at Lily's house. "Night after night, she would fly through his window and feast on his blood."

In spite of myself, I gulped, and also glanced out the window. "That never happened." My voice came out as a whisper. "And?"

Lightning streaked across the sky.

"Billy didn't know it at the time, but she was slowly turning him into a vampire." He held up three fingers. "Three bites is all it takes." He shrugged. "Well, that's if they don't decide to just kill and devour you instead. It really could go either way."

"I—it's not that I believe you, but . . . what happened?"

Tommy slowly turned to me. His expression turned serious. "First, he grew sensitive to the sun. Next, the smell of garlic bothered him. Then, he started getting a thirst . . . for blood! By the time he finally figured out what was happening, it was too late. He became one of the undead."

"And?"

He pretended to hammer something. "His parents had no choice but to put a stake through his heart."

I waved him away. "Okay, you just lost me. That's a stupid story."

"Why's it stupid?"

"Because it doesn't make any sense. I don't care if he was a vampire or not, what kind of parent would put a stake through their own child's heart?"

"Devin!"

Tommy and I jumped and whirled around to see Mom standing in the doorway.

She frowned. "What's the matter with you two?"

I pointed to the window. "Nothing, Mom. It's the thunder, and then we started talking about some horror movie we saw."

"I warned you not to watch those things. Devin, you know how scared you get."

Tommy nodded. "I know, Aunt Megan. I was just telling him that."

She walked over and patted his head. "Thank you, Tommy. I'm glad one of you has some sense."

"Oh, brother," I muttered. "What did you want, Mom?"

"Oh, that's right. I wanted you to know that I spoke to Lily's dad, and they're coming over for coffee and cake tomorrow night after dinner."

Tommy whipped his head in my direction. His eyes widened.

"They are?" I asked. "When did this happen?"

"Just now," she said. "I called him. Why? What's the big deal?"

"Uh, are you sure that's a good idea? We barely know them."

She cocked her head. "What's to know? They're new neighbors and we never really introduced ourselves. It's long overdue."

"But Mom . . ."

"Oh, I know what this is about." She walked over and pinched my cheek. "Don't worry, I won't embarrass you."

"It's not about that," I said.

She smirked. "C'mon, now. I saw the way you and Lily hit it off. I'm not blind."

"Like bats?" Tommy asked.

I glared at him.

Mom bent down and looked into my eyes. "Relax. I won't say anything bad. Lily is a lovely girl. I think you have very good taste."

"I bet Lily will think Devin has good taste too," Tommy said.

I sighed. "Not now, Tommy." I turned back to her. "Is there anything else, Mom?"

She studied me for a moment, and frowned. "I thought you would've been more excited." A look, like she was figuring something out, spread across her face. "Oh, I know what this is. I guess you have to play it cool in front of your mother. You know, I was your age too, once upon a time, so I know how it is. But this is the first girl you like, so enjoy the moment. One day, you'll look back at this as a distant, fond memory. Remember, nobody stays young forever."

"Well, Devin might," Tommy said.

"Tommy!" I yelled.

Mom glared at me. "Stop yelling at your cousin!"

Tommy nodded. "Thank you, Aunt Megan."

"My pleasure, Tommy." She walked toward the door. "Well, I'll leave the two of you alone now." She turned back to us and wagged her finger. "But no more scary movies!" She walked out.

I waited until I heard her footsteps on the staircase, then turned to Tommy. "What's the matter with you?"

"What? You should be thanking me! I'm trying to help you."

"You'd be helping me a lot more by cutting it out."

He thrust his finger in my face. "I can't do that! You don't have much time. We need to act fast."

"I don't want you doing anything."

He shook his head. "No, not me."

"What do you mean?"

He leaned in. "I thought of something while your mom was talking."

"That you're annoying?"

"No, I realized something else. Vampires are magical beings."

"Yeah, so?"

He spread his arms. "Duh, it's so obvious. The best way to defeat a magical being is with *another* magical being."

My face fell. "Oh, no . . ."

"Oh, yes. We keep forgetting." He pointed out the window. "You have a warlock living right across the street from you."

"No! There's no way I'm asking—"

"You have to!" Tommy cut me off. "Because your life may depend on it." He walked over to the window and looked out. "We need to ask Herb."

Thunder boomed across the sky.

CHAPTER THREE

FIGHTING MAGIC WITH MAGIC

The stupid picture with the Easter Bunny took a lot longer than I expected. Hours longer. To make matters worse, there were bunnies *everywhere*. It was like everyone at the mall forgot that there had been a magical bunny attack only months earlier.

By the time we got out of there, it was the middle of the afternoon. At least the day was gorgeous. Bright sun, very little breeze, and fresh air.

So why did I feel a chill walking up the path to Herb's house?

It was like I was being followed, but every time I turned to look there was nobody there.

I paused in front of his home. Even after all this time the sight of his gray, two-story house scared me.

It wasn't the wall of hedges that surrounded it. I don't even think it was that dark cloud, which always seemed to be hovering above.

It was just this feeling that something weird was lurking inside. And knowing Herb, I'd have to say that was a pretty accurate guess. Because, really, there was *nobody* weirder than him.

Tommy, of course, was oblivious to all of it.

"Are you sure this is a good idea?" I asked.

He continued walking without looking back. "Of course it's a good idea. I already told you a vampire is a magical being, and that it takes magic to fight magic."

"Where'd you get that from, Scooby-Doo?"

"You always ask me that, and if you ever bothered to watch any episodes, you'd probably learn a thing or two from them." He rang the bell.

The *Addams Family* theme played.

I sighed. "I'm just saying that you seem to be forgetting that Herb tried to kill us once."

Tommy rolled his eyes. "Are you ever going to let that go?" He knocked on the door. "And besides, he didn't really try to kill us. The Cuddle Bunnies did."

"And *who* created the Cuddle Bunnies?"

"Wow, you really hold a grudge, don't you?"

The door creaked open.

Herb stood there wearing a T-shirt with a picture of

an alligator eating an orange on the front. Underneath the gator it read, FLORIDA! A STATE WITH BITE! He smiled at us. "Howdy, boys, what can I do you for?"

I stared at him. "Why are you so tan?"

Herb glanced down at his arms. "Oh, I just came back from two glorious weeks in the Sunshine State for a little R and R and R. That means rest, relaxation, and . . ." He winked. "Romance."

I frowned. The thought of *anyone* liking Herb churned my stomach. "Romance?"

He nodded. "Of course! It was the annual Witches and Warlocks Conference in Fort Lauderdale. It felt like I was on spring break with Frankie and Annette!"

"What?" I asked.

Herb smiled. "It was oodles of fun! And, while I admit I'm no Burt Reynolds, I'm still known as something of a ladies' man around those parts." He brushed his remaining strands of hair over his head.

"Who?" I asked.

Herb's eyes widened. "Oh, where are my manners? You came over for a visit, and I'm keeping you at the front door. Come on in!" He stepped back.

"No, Herb," I said. "We really don't want to bother you. We just had a couple of questions, and—"

Herb waved dismissively. "Nonsense. There's always time for being neighborly. And besides, I bought gifts for you." He motioned us inside.

27

I shook my head. "We really don't have time, we're just here because—"

"You got us gifts?" Tommy barged past Herb into the house.

I sighed. "Of course."

Herb turned and followed him in. "Come on in, Devin! But shut the door behind you. We don't want Wendigo getting out."

"Yeah, we'd hate to lose your creepy cat," I muttered, stepping in and shuting the door behind me.

By the time I turned back around, Herb and Tommy were gone.

I made my way through the dark hallway until I reached the kitchen.

Tommy was already sitting and eating something.

"These are delicious!" he said, through a mouthful of whatever it was.

Herb smiled. "That's my world-famous Herbberry pie."

"What's a Herbberry?" Tommy asked.

Herb arched an eyebrow. "Uh, uh, uh. That's the secret ingredient."

I rolled my eyes. I had no idea what was worse, Herb trying to kill us or him being nice. Either way, he got on my nerves. "Yeah . . . so, anyway, the reason why we're here, is—"

Herb held up his index finger. "Oh, hold that thought!" He ran out of the kitchen.

I sat next to Tommy. "Is there going to be one time that we come here and you don't raid his fridge?"

"This was already out. And besides, it's delicious."

"I don't care what it is. We're not here to eat. We're here to ask some questions and get out as fast as we can. This place still gives me the creeps."

He cut off a bite of pie with his fork and held it up to me. "C'mon, you have to try this."

I swatted his hand away. "I don't want to try it!"

He took another bite. "This is the best Herbberry pie I've ever had."

"It's the only Herbberry pie you've ever had! And you want to know why? Because there's no such thing as Herbberry. He made it up. It's not a real ingredient."

"All of a sudden you're an expert baker?"

"He just used his name. That's all there was to it."

He shrugged and shoved another bite into his mouth. "It's still good, though."

"Here we are!" Herb rushed back into the room carrying a shopping bag. His creepy black cat was right on his heels.

The cat jumped onto the table, turned to me, and hissed.

I shrank back in my seat.

Herb grabbed the cat and tossed him to the ground. "No, Wendigo! These are our friends now!" He turned to us and shielded his mouth from the cat. "You'll have to forgive him, he senses your distrust of magical beings."

Tommy clucked his tongue at me. "That's not nice, Devin."

I looked back and forth between them. I wasn't sure who annoyed me more. *"What are you talking about?* I don't distrust magical beings!"

Herb smiled. "It's okay, Devin. I'm not offended. You've led a very sheltered life. I'm sure it's just that you haven't come across many magical beings."

I threw my hands up. "Why are we listening to a cat?"

Herb arched an eyebrow. "You don't like cats either?"

"Devin!" Tommy snapped.

My head started to pound. "This is ridiculous!"

Herb laughed. "I'm just joshing with you. He didn't say anything. He just doesn't like you. Now, where were we?"

Tommy pointed at the shopping bag. "You were about to give us gifts."

"Oh, yes! I almost forgot." Herb reached into the bag and pulled out a couple of T-shirts and tossed them to us.

I opened mine up. It was the same stupid, orange-eating gator T-shirt that he was wearing.

"I thought they were the most adorable things. And now we can all wear them together to neighborhood barbecues and whatnot. Everyone will be so jealous of all of us."

I forced a weak smile. "Yeah, I'm sure there's nothing that people want more than a novelty T-shirt."

Tommy slipped his over his head. "I'm going to wear mine now!" He pushed his arms through the sleeves until the shirt was over what he was already wearing.

Herb clapped. "Splendid!" He held his index finger up. "Oh, and there's one more thing!" He started laughing. "These are the best things ever. When I saw them, they were as good as bought." He reached into the bag again, fished out two bottles, and pushed them across the table toward us.

I picked one up and saw a tiny bit of sand and shells in one. "Bottled Florida Sunshine?"

Herb dabbed at his eyes and laughed. "Isn't that the funniest? Can you imagine? *Bottled sunshine?* It's like the Pet Rock all over again."

"What?" I asked.

"What will they think of next?" Herb said.

I had no idea what he was talking about, and it took every ounce of willpower I had not to roll my eyes. "Thanks, Herb. These are really great, but—"

"Oh, don't mention it. As Dionne Warwick says, that's what friends are for."

"Um . . . yeah. Anyway—"

Herb slid the bag across the table. "There are three other sets inside, for your parents and dear little Abby. We're all going to be the talk of the town!"

"I have no doubt about it," I muttered.

Herb sat back in his seat. "Anyhoo, what brings you boys around?"

I stuffed the shirt and bottles back into the over-sized shopping bag. "That's what we've been trying to tell you."

Tommy looked back over one shoulder, then the other, like he was checking to see if anyone was listening. "We need your help."

"Anything, boys," Herb said. "You can always count on Herb. It's my motto. Now, what's the trouble?"

Tommy leaned forward. "What do you know about vampires?"

Herb's expression changed. The smile disappeared from his face. "Why do you ask about vampires?"

Tommy glanced at me. "Because Devin's in love with one."

"I'm not in love! I barely know her. And anyway, she's not a vampire. There are no such things as vampires."

Herb looked slowly back and forth between us. "Oh, there are vampires."

Tommy elbowed me. "I told you!"

"What are you talking about?" I asked.

Herb pyramided his fingers in front of his face. "There are vampires. And they're deadly. Though I haven't seen one in quite some time."

Tommy gulped. "You've met some, for real?"

Herb nodded. "Oh, yes. Barely escaped with my life the last time."

I swallowed hard. "Herb, we don't have time for—"

"I was visiting Transylvania," Herb said. "For one of those Witches and Warlocks conferences. Well, as you well may know, Transylvania is also famous for vampires. Now I don't need to tell you that warlocks and vampires don't mix. They're like Martin and Lewis right around the breakup, not the reconciliation on the telethon."

I held my hand up. "Herb, I have no idea what you're talking about. And besides, we don't know that she's a vampire. Tommy just thinks that she is."

Tommy laughed. "Oh, she's a vampire all right. She's really pretty and she's talking to Devin? I mean, c'mon!" He turned to me. "No offense."

"Gee, Tommy, why would I take offense at that?" I yelled.

Herb clapped. "Boys!"

Tommy and I looked back at Herb.

"We need to focus." He peered over his glasses at us. "We have no time for bickering. If true, this is serious. Vampires are no laughing matter. Sure, some people think they're funny and quick with a quip, like George Hamilton, but they're not. They're really more like Bela Lugosi."

"Who?" I asked.

Herb ignored me. "Where's this one?"

Tommy pointed. "Down the block."

Herb glanced toward the window. "Oh, dear. That's not good at all." He gazed out. "Are you sure?"

Tommy nodded. "She only comes out at night."

"She goes to private school," I said.

Tommy snorted. "On weekends?"

Herb rubbed his chin. "Hmmm . . . that doesn't mean anything by itself, but it's something to keep an eye on. What else?"

"Trust me, she's a vampire," Tommy said. "A blood-sucking, soul-stealing vampire. And we've never even seen her dad . . . well, except for that coffin he sleeps in."

Herb leaned forward. "Coffin?"

"We don't know that he sleeps in it!" I said. "And besides, he collects movie memorabilia."

"Oh, please," Tommy said. "You're just going by what the movers said." His mouth drooped. "I just thought of something. I bet you he's the lead vampire. The one pulling all the strings. He's the one we have to kill."

"We're not killing anyone!" I yelled.

Tommy pounded his fist on the table. "Herb, please tell him that we have to kill the neighbor."

Herb held up his hand, motioning for silence. He stood up and paced the room.

"What's wrong?" I asked.

"If there are indeed vampires here, we must tread carefully." He sighed. "Nothing can ruin a town like vampires. They really bring down property values."

Tommy shot me an I-told-you-so look. "See?" He turned to Herb. "Do you think you can whip up some spell that'll turn them all into dust, or something like that?"

Herb shook his head. "I'm afraid not. Vampires are notoriously immune to witch or warlock magic. I might be able to do something, but indirectly. If this is true, we'll have to figure out more conventional means."

"This is stupid," I said. "Do you two hear your-selves? There are no such things as vampires, and even if there were, we don't know that Lily is one."

Herb stopped pacing. "Her name is Lily?"

The way he asked made me nervous. "Yeah, so?"

"Not good. Lily is a common vampire name. It's like Smith and Jones for mortals. Or Shirley for goblins."

"Goblins?" I asked.

Herb thrust his index finger into the air. "This bears further checking. We need to be able to rule it out, or address it." He rubbed his chin again. "Now, I need to think of a pretext to meet them and see for myself."

Tommy jumped up. "You don't need a reason. Devin's mom invited them over for coffee and cake tonight."

Herb whipped his head in our direction. "To your house?"

I nodded slowly, not liking the way he said it. "Uh . . . yeah?"

Herb rushed over to me and grabbed my shoulders. "Devin, you must not let them into your house!" He let go. "At least, not until we figure out what they are."

"It's too late for that," Tommy said. "She already invited them . . . kind of."

"What does 'kind of' mean?" Herb asked.

Tommy thought a moment. "It means she invited them over, but not actually into the house. I don't know if that counts or not. She's not really good with these sorts of things."

Herb's brow furrowed. "Hmmm . . . I don't know if that counts, either, but until we do know we must take precautions."

"Herb," I said. "I don't really think that's neces—"

He held his hand up again. "No, I insist! You rest easy, my young friend. And don't worry about a thing. Herbert T. Dorfman is on the case!"

For some reason, that didn't make me feel any better.

CHAPTER FOUR

MEETING THE NEIGHBORS

As far back as I can remember, every single time Mom's invited company over, I've hated it. The people were boring, and even worse, Abby and I were forced to be nice to each other for the entire night. The worst one was probably the first time Herb came by. After that, I never wanted to have any guests over ever again. Until now.

This time, I had to admit, I was kind of excited about seeing Lily. I'd wanted to speak to her for months, and now she was actually coming over to my house. Finally, something good was going my way.

Well, unless you consider the fact that she just might be a vampire, a possibility that Tommy wasn't letting me forget.

He was sitting on the edge of my bed, writing in my

notebook, which he had now changed to the Vampire Research File. "Okay, I assume you still have no holy water?"

I shook my head. "No, and we've been through this a thousand times already. I don't know why you think that every person in town has a supply of holy water in their house."

He scribbled in the notebook. "Because when you live in Gravesend, it should really be a requirement. When I'm an adult, I'm going to make sure that my home is always fully stocked. As far as I'm concerned, you can never have too much holy water." He glanced at my clock. "Hmmm. There's no time to go and get anything blessed before they get here. By the time I'd get there and back she'll probably have your blood half-drained." He shrugged. "I mean, I could probably stop them, but by that point what difference would it make? We'd better come up with an alternate plan."

I pictured my blood being drained from my body and winced. "Why is it that every time you say something about what might happen it involves me dying?"

"I'm sorry, but I don't have time to make things all nice and sweet for you. This is serious, and the sooner you realize it the better off you'll be." He stood up and peered out my window. "Now, where the heck is Herb? He's supposed to be here already."

"Yeah, and that's another thing. I still don't

understand why we had to include him. He's just going to make things worse."

"Do you even pay attention when I talk?"

I shook my head. "I try not to."

Tommy ignored me. "Magic to fight magic, remember?"

"Yeah, but Herb told you that vampires are immune to warlock magic."

He snapped his fingers. "Aha! So, you admit that she's a vampire!"

"No, I didn't say that." I rubbed my temples. "I don't know what I'm saying. You're giving me a headache."

"Better a headache now than a neckache later. If you know what I mean."

I walked away from him. "Please promise me that you're not going to do any of this while Lily's around, okay?"

Tommy followed me. "I don't know why you even want her. Relationships with vampires don't work out. Seriously, what if you wind up marrying her? You know how uncomfortable it is to sleep in a coffin? It's also very claustrophobic."

I pushed him away. "Nobody said anything about getting married. I just don't want any of this talk."

"But we have to find out whether or not she's a vampire."

"No, we don't. Your plans are stupid. And what's

worse, you never even let me in on them. I never have any idea what you're doing"

His expression turned serious. "Did you know that vampires can read minds?"

"No, they can't. And she's not a vampire."

"They can. That's why I try to keep some things from you so they can't read your mind and discover our plan. Because, no offense, but between the two of us you're kind of the weak link."

I tapped my chest. *"I'm the weak link?"*

"I said, no offense."

"Okay, again, just because you say 'no offense' doesn't mean it's okay!"

He frowned. "Wow, you sure are sensitive lately."

"Devin!" Mom called from downstairs.

For once, I was grateful for her interruption. Anything to get a small break from Tommy.

"Yeah, Mom?" I shouted.

"Why don't you and Tommy come down and help me set up?"

"Okay!" I started toward the door.

Tommy ran in front of me. "What are you doing?"

"What do you mean, what am I doing? Didn't you just hear her? She wants us to come down and help."

"But it's your mom's fault that we're in this mess to begin with. Tell her you're busy now."

"What should I tell her? That we can't help since we're planning for vampires?"

He thought a moment. "Do you think she'll be okay with that?"

"No, I don't think she'll be okay! Let's go." I motioned for him to follow.

I walked out of my room. Thankfully, Tommy came along without too much objection and followed me down the steps.

Around halfway down I heard talking.

"Please, won't you come in?" Mom's voice.

I froze. My heart pounded. I didn't know if it was because I was happy or scared. Or maybe a little bit of both.

Tommy grabbed my arm and whispered. "She let them in! Your mom let them in!"

My hand trembled. I hated that Tommy was getting to me with this. "Maybe it's Herb."

"We both know it's not Herb!" He tugged at my arm. "C'mon, let's go back upstairs."

"We can't. We're already too far down!"

"We're not ready yet!" Tommy insisted.

"Devin, is that you?" Mom called again.

I winced. "Uh, yeah, Mom."

"What are you doing? Come on down, already!" she said.

I pulled Tommy's arm off me. "C'mon, we have to go."

He put his hand in front of my chest. "Wait! Did you ever stop to consider that your mom might be compromised? We might have to stake her."

I swatted his hand away. "Will you stop with that? We're not staking my mom." I took another step down. "Now let's go!"

I continued down the stairs and turned the corner for the living room.

Mom, Dad, and Abby were on one couch, while Lily was on the other.

I stopped in my tracks, staring at her.

My body went numb.

She smiled.

My heart flipped.

Tommy leaned over and whispered, "I'll go get the garlic."

"Shut up," I said, out the side of my mouth.

Mom saw me. "Oh, there you are!" She stood up and gestured to Lily. "I actually invited Lily and her dad over earlier than I told you." She threw her hands up. "Surprise!"

My eyes darted around the room. "Her dad?"

Suddenly, someone stood up from the reclining chair.

I hadn't even noticed anyone sitting in it, since it was facing away from me.

Instinctively, I jumped back.

There might've even been a small shriek, though I'm not sure. And I also couldn't tell if it came from me or from Tommy.

All I knew was that I had my hands curled into fists and bunched up around my throat.

I felt like a fool, which wasn't helped whatsoever by the fact that Tommy was huddled behind me with his arms covering his neck.

"Devin, what are you doing?" Mom asked.

The man in front of us laughed. "Oh, it's okay. I must've startled them."

Tommy and I stared up at a towering man with dark hair that had a few gray streaks running through the sides. He must've been well over six feet tall.

He was wearing a dark suit with a red shirt.

My first thought was that he was way too dressed up for a night of coffee and cake at our house.

He extended his hand. "You must be Devin!"

"Devin," Mom said, "this is Mr. Moroi, Lily's dad."

I reached out slowly. "Hi."

He grasped my hand.

I don't know if he was squeezing hard on purpose, but it sure felt like it. My hand felt like Play-Doh in his grip.

"None of that Mr. Moroi stuff," he said. "Please, call me Levi."

I didn't answer, only nodded instead.

When he finally released my hand I had to flex it several times to stop the pain.

He turned to Tommy. "And that must make you Tommy." He extended his hand again.

Tommy just waved. "Hey."

"Why doesn't everyone sit down?" Mom said.

"Devin, aren't you going to sit next to Lily?" Abby practically sang.

I glared at her but she only smirked back at me.

Lily smiled. "Sure. Come sit here, Devin."

I nodded again and slowly walked to the couch. I knew it had to be my imagination, but the closer I got to her, the better I felt. I sat next to her.

Mom cocked her head. "Tommy, aren't you going to join us?"

He pointed to the ground. "No, I'm good over here."

"Tommy!" she snapped. She turned to Dad and swatted his arm. "Will you tell the boys to stop acting so weird?"

"Don't act weird, boys," he said.

Mom sighed. "Go sit down, Tommy."

Tommy took a few steps and turned, so he was facing Levi, and sidestepped the rest of the way. He looked like a nervous crab. He sat on the other side of me, but scooted to the far end of the couch.

Mom stared at him and then turned back to Levi. "I'm sorry, they're not usually like this."

"They're not?" Dad asked.

Mom peeked at him through the corner of her eye before pointing to the coffee table in the center, where everything was already laid out. "Please, help yourselves."

Everyone reached out and started taking food, except me and Tommy.

He motioned toward Levi and flapped his hands like a bat.

"Stop it," I mouthed at him.

Mom gestured to Lily's dad. "Levi was just about to tell us all about his performing arts school. He's the headmaster there."

Levi took a sip and set his cup down. "Before I do that, are you sure you're done with your story about the water recycling project you did for the town?"

"Yes!" Mom cut in, probably a little too fast. "Yes, he's done."

Dad frowned. "I guess so."

I stared at Levi. As much as I hated to admit it, Tommy's words kept sneaking into my mind. Could he be a vampire? He seemed so nice.

Suddenly, Lily's leg pressed against mine for a moment, and that's all it took. I couldn't focus on anything else. It was like there was a mini-sun shining on that one spot.

The doorbell rang.

Mom turned toward it. "Who could that be?"

Tommy glanced at me. "On my signal," he whispered.

I shook my head. "No! No signal!"

Mom stood up. "I'll get it."

As soon as she walked out of the room, Tommy turned to Levi. "I have a question!"

Levi smiled. Wow, his teeth were bright. "Yes?"

Tommy banged his index fingers together, like a cross. "Um, can you tell us about your school?"

Levi didn't react to the cross whatsoever. "Of course."

Tommy turned to me, shrugged, and whispered, "I thought that would work."

"Just stop," I said out the side of my mouth.

"Well," Levi said. "The Nosfer Academy of Talented Understudies is one of the premier acting schools in the country."

"It's strange that I've never heard of it," Dad said.

Levi leaned back in his chair. "We're very exclusive. We only want a select few. Those who can fly above the rest, if you will."

"And you want Devin?" Abby blurted.

Levi laughed. "The whole purpose of the dinner and dance is to drum up interest in a few special kids we would like to enroll. If they like what they see, perhaps they'll join us, and if they don't, then no harm done. We all enjoy a good meal and call it a night."

Tommy leaned forward. "Will there be any garlic in the meal?"

Levi shrugged. "I don't ask the chef what he uses for ingredients."

"I hope so," Tommy said. "Because I love garlic. Do you?"

"Depends on the dish," Levi said.

"Is there any reason why we're discussing cooking?" Dad cut in.

Tommy shook his head. "No, just curious."

Dad's eyes ping-ponged back and forth between Tommy and me before finally turning back to Levi. "Sorry about that. I wish I could say that this was unusual, but it's not."

"Oh, it's quite all right. I was a kid once, many hundreds of years ago." Levi laughed again.

"So, I heard that you're very big in the theater?" Dad asked.

Levi placed his hand on his chest. "Not as big as I used to be, but I've been in many Broadway shows, national productions, and an occasional movie. Though I'm probably much bigger overseas in the European market. But now I've decided to give back. That's why I run a school, to train the next generation."

"That's very nice of you," Dad said. "Just curious, is there a lot of money to be made in running a school?"

"I don't do it for the money. I do it for my love of

theater. That's one of the reasons why we're having this event. A theater always needs actors. They're its lifeblood." He glanced at me.

Wait . . . what did he say?

Mom came back into the room. "Look who's here!"

Herb walked in behind her. "Howdy, neighbors!"

Mom dragged a chair over from the dining room table. "Here you go, Herb."

He took it from her. "Thank you, I've always depended on the kindness of strangers." He laughed. "Not that you're a stranger, but then again, I'm no Blanche Dubois."

I turned to Tommy and mouthed, "Who?"

He shrugged.

Herb and Mom sat.

Mom pointed to Herb. "Levi, this is our neighbor Herb Dorfman. Herb, this is Levi Moroi and his daughter, Lily."

Herb cocked his head. "Did you say Moroi? What an unusual name."

Levi nodded. "Yes, it's European."

"Transylvanian," Tommy whispered.

"Shut up," I whispered back.

"What brings you over, Herb?" Dad asked.

"Oh, uh . . . Devin mentioned that new neighbors were coming over, and you know me. Nobody's more neighborly than Herbert T. Dorfman, where in this case, the T stands for 'Time to make the new neighbors feel welcome.'"

Levi bowed. "That is very kind of you."

"Levi was just telling us about his acting school," Mom said.

"Acting!" Herb shouted. "Why, I'm no Marlon Brando, but I've dabbled as a thespian in my time."

"Who?" I asked.

"That's great to hear," Levi said. "Perhaps your child would like to check out our school as well. We're having a dinner and dance this Friday night."

"Oh, I don't have any children. I seem to be always locked in eligible bachelor status."

Levi arched an eyebrow. "No children and no spouse? Well, at least you don't have to account for your whereabouts to someone all the time." He rubbed his hands together. "You know what? Why don't you come out Friday as well? We're always looking for qualified chaperones, and you seem overly qualified."

"Herb's getting to go to the dance, too?" Abby asked. "And I can't?"

"You're not going," I said.

Lily touched my hand. Jolts shot through me. "I think we're going to have a lot of fun at this dance, Devin. It'll be a great way to get to know each other better."

I opened my mouth to speak, but no words came out, so I just nodded. Her perfume started to reach me.

I was dizzy, but in a good way. I couldn't recognize the scent, but it seemed familiar. Like something from when I was younger.

"Everybody's going to the dance but me!" Abby yelled. "I want to go, too!"

"You're not going!" I repeated.

"She can take my place," Tommy muttered.

"That's not fair!" Abby said.

"I'd love to chaperone," Herb said. He reached into his pocket, fished out his phone, and held it up in front of his face. "Let me just get your number, and—" He fumbled with the phone for a few seconds, and then stopped and peered over the screen. He looked back to the phone and dropped it.

It crashed to the floor, followed by the unmistakable sound of glass breaking.

Herb stared straight ahead at Levi. His mouth hung open.

Levi's eyes narrowed. "Is everything all right?"

Herb nodded slowly for a moment, before finally speaking. "Yes. Uh . . . yes. Just a little clumsy, is all." He reached down to pick up his phone and twirled it in his hands. "I guess my screen cracked."

Levi bolted up from his seat. "Well, I'm afraid we have to go."

Lily stood as well.

My heart dropped. I didn't want her to leave.

"So soon?" Mom asked. "But you only just got here."

Levi walked over to her and grasped her hand. "In the theater, nighttime is when everything comes alive. We have a special performance planned for Friday night, which Lily has to rehearse for."

Lily nodded. "I can't wait for you to see it, Devin." She smiled at me.

Just hearing her say my name made me dizzy.

Levi bent and kissed Mom's hand. "Thank you again for having us."

"Oh, my!" Mom said. "Well, you're welcome here anytime."

Levi smiled wide. His teeth were definitely whiter than I've ever seen on anyone. "Now that we have an invitation, you won't be able to get rid of us."

They both laughed.

"But call first," Dad said.

Levi shook Dad's hand and then turned to Herb. "I'm sure we'll also be seeing a lot of each other."

Herb didn't say anything.

"And I'll get in touch about chaperoning," Levi said. "Since your phone is broken, let me give you my card." He reached into his pocket, took out a card, and handed it to Herb.

Herb pinched it between his fingers and pulled it quickly back.

"I'll walk you out," Mom said.

Lily turned to me and smiled. "Can't wait to see more of you, Devin."

My heart felt like it would explode any moment. "I can't either." I winced. Should I have said that?

Mom walked out of the room with Levi and Lily. Abby tagged along after them.

"I think I'd better get going, as well," Herb said.

"You sure, Herb?" Dad asked.

"Yes, I, uh . . . have some things I need to take care of." His face looked pale.

"Okay, that's too bad," Dad said. "Well, you can show yourself out, right?" Dad looked back over his shoulder to check for Mom. "In that case, I'm going upstairs before your mom gets me to help her clean up. If she asks, tell her I'm on a very important call for work." He bolted from the room and up the stairs.

Herb waited a moment, until we heard Dad's door close. He rushed over to us and held up his cracked phone.

"What's going on?" Tommy asked.

Herb glanced at the door before continuing. He leaned in and whispered, "When I took out the phone to get his number, I tried to discreetly take a picture of them."

"And?" I asked.

Herb closed his eyes a moment. "I snapped one without their knowing."

I shrugged. "So?"

"When I looked at it, they weren't in the picture. They have no reflection. They're vampires."

CHAPTER FIVE

VAMPIRE PREP

For the last half-hour I had done nothing but watch Tommy preparing for the night. So far he'd put duct tape in the shape of crosses all over my windows and arranged several cloves of garlic by the door.

I'd passed by open sewers that smelled better than my room.

I waved my hand in front of my nose. "This is ridiculous. I'll never be able to fall asleep with all this stink."

"Better a little smell than a vampire midnight snack."

"We don't even know for sure that she's a vampire."

He waved dismissively. "Please, you heard what Herb said."

"I know, but we're just supposed to take his word for it? He couldn't even show us any proof because his phone cracked."

"Yeah, but why would he lie about them not showing up in any pictures?"

"I'm not saying he's lying. But you also have to remember that he's old. He might not know how to use his phone the right way. That happens to my parents all the time."

"He said he took the picture and didn't see them afterwards. Not all of us, *them*! He didn't see *them*!"

"I know, but—"

"No buts!" Tommy said. "We need to be safe. Did you know that vampires always seek out the cleverest members in a group? Those are the ones they try to turn. Because they figure that those are the ones who can change everyone else."

I shook my head. "That's not true."

He ignored me and kept talking. "And no offense to everyone in your family, but I don't think there's anyone else here even *worth* changing."

"Again, just because you say 'no offense' doesn't mean that it's not offensive."

"All I'm saying is that if I were you, I'd be very careful tonight." He reached into his backpack and pulled out a small container.

"What's that?"

He opened it and started sprinkling the contents on the floor.

"Hey!" I rushed over and grabbed his arm. "What are you doing?"

He looked at me. "What? It's garlic powder."

"Why are you sprinkling garlic powder on my floor?"

He looked at me like I was nuts. "Uh, because your mom's out of regular garlic. This is all she had in the kitchen." He pulled his arm away. "Now let me finish."

I watched him sprinkle the powder around my bed, his sleeping bag, and the windows and pictured just how much trouble I was going to be in when Mom saw it. "Will you stop already? I think that's enough."

"I can't! We need all of it. If they get past the window, this is the last line of defense we have around where we sleep. You can never be too careful with vampires."

I pictured just how messy this was going to wind up being. "Yeah, but then we're going to have to clean all this up."

He waved his hand at me. "Yeah, don't worry. We will."

I already knew what that meant. I'd be left doing everything myself.

Tommy searched around my room. He went to the dresser and lifted the bottles of Florida Sunshine Herb gave me. "Maybe we can use these?"

"Are you kidding me? Those are novelty gifts, like the stupid T-shirts he bought."

"They can't label it as Florida sunshine if it isn't true. People would sue the company for false advertising."

I grabbed the bottle from him and held it up in front

of his face. "It's a bottle! That's it!" I put it back on the dresser. "Now think of something else."

There was a knock at the door.

I whipped my head toward the sound. "Oh, no . . ."

"Devin?"

I exhaled. "Yeah, Dad?"

He opened the door. "I just want to say . . ." He stopped speaking. His nose wrinkled. "What the heck is that smell?" He looked down and waved in front of his face. "What's that stuff around your bed?"

I followed his gaze and pointed. "That stuff?"

He nodded. "Yeah, that stuff."

I tried to remain expressionless. "It's garlic powder."

"Uh-huh." He stared at me for a moment. "May I ask why you have garlic powder sprinkled all around your room?"

"Mosquitoes," Tommy said.

Dad's eyes narrowed. "Mosquitoes?"

Tommy nodded. "Yeah, this keeps them away. It's a very bad time of year for them. Their mating season and all."

Dad leaned back and peered into the hallway before turning back to us. "Okay, I don't know what's going on, but thankfully, your mother's in bed right now or there'd be murder. Probably mine." He waved his arm across the room. "So, I don't care what you do tonight about mosquitoes, bedbugs, or whatever other reason you have for putting garlic powder all over. You want to sleep with that stuff around, that's fine. All I know is that it reeks in here, and this better be all cleaned up by morning." He took a step out the door, stopped, and turned back in. "And one more thing. If your mother yells, I knew nothing about this, understand?"

We nodded.

"Good." He looked at us once more, shook his head, and walked out.

I grabbed Tommy's arm. "Mosquitoes? Is that the best you could do?"

"He bought it, didn't he? Or did you want me to tell him vampires?"

"I don't know what I wanted you to tell him, but saying mosquitoes is stupid."

"You have to realize that right now we're protecting your family. Until we know for sure what's going on, there's no need to panic anyone else."

"But you told me that you *did* know for sure."

He shrugged. "Well, I kind of do, but there's always that little bit of doubt. Anyway, they're not the ones who need to worry." He pointed to me. "You are. Remember, vampires will seek out the smartest, and since they know I'm not part of your immediate family, the next one in line is you."

"There's no way they would pick you over me."

"Let's agree to disagree on that. Either way, though, we have to be ready. I suggest we take shifts sleeping."

"Seriously?"

"Of course! We can't go to sleep knowing there are bloodthirsty vampires right across the street, just waiting for the chance to come in here and either feast on us or turn us into their soulless, zombie slaves, right?"

"Well, no, but—"

"No buts. That settles it. We're sleeping in shifts. I'll take first watch while you sleep."

"How long is each shift?"

"Let's say two hours." He walked to the closet and rooted around a moment, then brought out a bat. "You don't have a wood bat?"

I shook my head. "Who has a wood bat? Nobody uses them anymore."

He looked it over and sighed. "Okay, I guess it'll have to do for tonight. But we need to start thinking about getting wooden stakes." He eyed my dresser and motioned toward it. "Do you think your mom will notice if we break off a piece and carve it into a point?"

"You're not doing that! Now, stop it and let's go to sleep." I clicked off the lights and jumped into bed. "I just want you to know that I bet everything will be fine in the morning."

"Of course it will be." He tapped his chest. "Because

I protected us. Now, get to sleep, because I'm getting you up in two hours for your shift."

I sighed. "Whatever."

Last thing I saw before I closed my eyes was Tommy pacing the floor, holding the bat up by his shoulder.

I blinked several times, until my eyes fluttered open. The sun seeped in through the windows. It was daytime. I sat up, took a look around, and rolled my eyes.

On the end of my bed, fast asleep, was Tommy.

I shoved him with my foot until he rolled off and crashed to the floor.

"Hey!" he yelled. "What'd you do that for?" He sat up and rubbed his head.

"You were sleeping! You said we were going to take shifts and you'd wake me in two hours. Instead, you went to sleep."

"So, I got a little tired. I wasn't asleep for that long. Maybe, an hour . . . two, tops." He reached up and felt his neck. "I don't feel anything, do you?"

I checked mine. "No, nothing. I told you this was stupid."

Tommy stood up. "What are you talking about? You should be thanking me instead."

"Thanking you?" I pointed all around the room. "Did you see all this? Now we have to clean it all up."

He shrugged. "First of all, the mess is a small price to pay for safety. And second, we're not cleaning it up! We can't. Not as long as they're out there."

I jumped off my bed. "So what do you want to do? Just keep it on my floor forever? How do you want to explain that to my mom?"

"She'd prefer vampires?"

"Okay, obviously they're not vampires. I think Herb was wrong." I smiled. "And that means Lily is okay."

The door barged open.

Tommy and I jumped.

Abby stormed in. "Devin, Mom's been calling you for over twenty minutes, and she's—" Abby stopped short and threw her hands up in front of her eyes. "Why is it so bright in here? Pull the shades down or something."

I glanced at Tommy, and only one thought went through my mind . . .

Uh oh.

CHAPTER SIX

ABBY IS A PAIN IN THE NECK

Over the years, Abby and I have gotten into many fights. Over toys. Over what to watch on TV. Over her annoying me. Really, over everything. But I had to admit that never, ever, did I think that we'd get into a fight about needing to check her neck for fang marks.

Abby swatted my hand away. "Leave me alone!"

I wrapped my arms around her. "Abby, will you hold still? We need to see something." I pinned her arms to her sides and turned to Tommy. "Look quickly!"

Abby wriggled, getting away. "Let go of me!"

I lost my grip and she whirled, clawing at my arms.

I grabbed her again. "Hurry up!"

"I'm trying! Hold her still."

Abby thrashed her arms, and I felt my hold loosen. "When the heck did she get so strong?"

"You know when!" Tommy said. "Now, hold her still!"

She squirmed. "LET. ME. GO!"

I clasped my hands around her. "Abby, one more second!"

She growled. It sounded almost like a wild animal. Her mouth opened and she lunged for me.

"She's trying to bite me!" I said. "Hurry up."

Tommy examined her neck. "Look, right there!" He pointed to two small, reddish dots on the side of her neck.

My heart dropped. "Oh, no."

Tommy nodded. "I told you."

I leaned in close. It was difficult to see, with the way she was fighting me, but they were there. "I can barely see them, though. How is that possible?"

"That's easy," Tommy said. "Vampire saliva has a natural sealant. Otherwise, the people that they're trying to turn would have these big gaping holes in their necks, and that would kind of give everything away. Not to mention make a big mess, with blood everywhere. Remember, vampires like to do everything on the hush-hush."

My hold on her eased up. "They kind of look a little like mosquito bites."

Tommy jabbed his finger at me. "And that's what makes them so sneaky!"

Abby elbowed me in the stomach.

"Oof!" I doubled over.

She spun around and kicked me in the shin. "I said, let go of me!"

"Ow!" I grabbed my leg and crumpled to the floor.

Abby ran out of the room. "*Mooooooooooooom!*"

I rubbed my shin. "Just great. Now how are we going to explain all this?"

Tommy held his hand up. "Don't worry, let me do all the talking."

"No! I don't want you to do all the talking. That's what always gets us into trouble." I stopped to think a moment. "Wait a second! Didn't you say the vampires would go after the smartest one?" I pointed toward the door. "*Abby?* Seriously?"

"Will you calm down?" He waved his arm around the room. "We had the garlic powder, remember? Everyone else had nothing. They had no choice but to go after Abby. You're lucky that I'm around."

I rolled my eyes. "Yeah, I feel really lucky. I have vampires right across the street who are now able to get into my house at any time." I pulled myself to my feet, still rubbing my shin. "Even worse, I have a little sister who might be a vampire? She already terrifies me as it is. Yeah, lucky me."

He smacked my face. "Calm down!"

"Ow!" I brought my hand up to my cheek. "What'd you do that for?"

"You're panicking, and I need you calm!"

"I wasn't panicking!" I punched his arm.

"Ow!" He rubbed the spot where I hit him.

"That was for hitting me."

He held hands out in front of him. "Okay, stop! We can't be turning on each other. This is the time we need to stick together." Tommy closed his eyes, took a deep breath, and exhaled. "I need to think." He started to pace. "Okay, get the VR File."

"Can't you just say it without needing to write it down?"

He stopped and turned to me. He gave me a look like he couldn't believe how stupid I was. "What's the point in having a VR File if we're not going to use it?"

I sighed. "Fine." I picked the notebook and a pen up off my dresser. "Happy?"

He didn't answer, and instead just picked up talking from where he'd left off.

"Okay, here's what we know." He counted off on his fingers. "One, your neighbors are vampires. Two, since your mom invited them, they can now get in whenever they want. Three, Abby's already been bitten once, which means she already has some vampire traits."

"Like what?"

He pointed at the window. "You already saw the sensitivity to sunlight. Soon, she'll have the same for certain smells. Increased strength. Oh, she'll also be sneaky."

"She's already sneaky."

"Well, then, sneakier. Possibly fangs, but I'm not really sure. I have to check that one out."

"Fangs?" I pictured Abby with sharp teeth, biting into my neck, and shivered. "So what do we do?"

He shrugged. "There's only one thing I can think of for right now."

"What's that?"

"I think we might have to eliminate her."

"Will you stop it, already? Why is your first thought always eliminating someone?"

"You can't be too careful with vampires."

"We're not eliminating her!" I stood up and peered out the door. "Do you really think that Abby is going to become one?" I gulped. "We can't let that happen. I have to do something."

"The main thing is we can't let her get bit again. I think with only one bite there's still hope to change her back, but if there's another one . . . I don't know." Tommy stepped out into the hall and looked around.

I followed him out. The hallway was clear. "What are you doing?"

"We have to try and keep Abby in our sights and see what she does. We can't leave her alone for too long. We need to follow her."

"You better not follow me!"

Tommy and I whirled toward the voice.

Abby was standing in the hallway. I could swear that she wasn't there before.

I'm embarrassed to say how long and loud our shriek was. And I was even more embarrassed when Dad came storming up the stairs and saw us.

"What's going on?" Dad yelled. He stopped in his tracks. "Why are you and Tommy crouching in the corner?"

Tommy and I looked at each other and stood up.

I stared at Abby. "Abby scared us."

Dad turned to her and pointed. "Abby did?"

I nodded. "Yeah, she just kind of appeared out of nowhere."

Tommy glanced at me.

Dad sighed. "Abby, don't scare your older brother and cousin."

Abby stomped her way toward me. "You started it!"

I backed up against the wall.

Abby thrust her finger in my face. "I'm warning you, Devin! You better not mess with me again, or I'll—"

I threw my arms up to cover my throat.

Thankfully, Dad stepped between us and pulled Abby away.

"Let's go, Abby," Dad said.

"Where are you going?" I asked.

"Abby was complaining about headaches this morning, and her eyes were bothering her, so we're going to go get it checked out."

"Nothing a good stake to the heart wouldn't cure," Tommy muttered.

I swatted his chest. "Shut up."

Dad pulled Abby toward the stairs.

She glared at me the whole way.

Was it my imagination, or were her eyes tinted red?

CHAPTER SEVEN

ELIMINATING THE SOURCE

We raced across the street to Herb's.

Again, I had the weird sensation of being watched, but every time I glanced over my shoulder there was nothing. The sun was shining brightly, which seemed to rule out any vampires, but unfortunately that didn't help get rid of the feeling. I tried to shake it off, but with each step I took up Herb's walkway it got stronger and stronger.

Tommy pressed the doorbell and held his finger there.

The *Addams Family* theme went off, again and again, but no answer.

"Maybe he's not home?" I said.

Tommy pounded on the door. "He's home. He's old, so he doesn't have anything to do, or a lot of friends.

Where else would he be? I don't know why he's ignoring us, though. Usually he can't wait for the chance to tell us his boring stories." He pounded again. "Herb, open up!"

Out of the corner of my eye, I saw movement from the window. I grabbed Tommy's shoulder and pointed. "There! I saw something moving inside!"

"What the heck is going on? Why is he hiding?" Tommy banged louder this time. "Herb, we see you in there! Open the door!"

The window shade fluttered.

"Stop knocking!" I said. "I just saw him."

We stayed quiet and listened.

I heard a sound from inside.

We pressed our ears to the door.

I heard a few creaks. There was definitely movement.

Tommy frowned. "He *is* hiding from us!" He knocked again. "Herb, we hear you in there! Open up!"

"Go away!" Herb shouted.

"Herb, c'mon!" I yelled. "I don't know what's going on, but it's important!"

The door finally creaked slightly open. Through the crack, I saw his eye.

"What do you want?" Herb asked.

"We need your help!" I said. "Abby's been bitten!"

His eye widened.

The door inched open a little more.

The smell hit me right away, and I reeled back.

Garlic.

Herb stood there staring at us. He was wearing a turtleneck sweater and a necklace of garlic cloves. He eyed us for a few moments. "How do I know you're not lying to me? For all I know, you could be like Chris Sarandon trying to use your charm to enter my home." He wagged his finger. "Well, I assure you, I'm just as equipped as Roddy McDowall was."

That was it. I'd had it. *"What are you talking about?"*

Herb's brow furrowed. "What I'm saying is—how do I know that either of you haven't been bitten and you're trying to use my good, kindhearted nature against me? Sure, I might seem as lovable as Jim Nabors to you, but believe you me, I know how to take care of myself."

"Herb, we're not vampires!" Tommy yelled.

"That's just what a vampire would say. Well, you're out of luck, creatures of the night." He sneered at us. "I didn't invite you in, so—"

I rolled my eyes. "Oh, for—" I shoved the door open and stormed past him.

Herb stared after me and shrugged. "Okay, I guess that works."

Tommy followed me in, and Herb slammed the door behind us.

He turned three different locks and checked the peephole before turning back toward us. "Were you followed?"

I thought about my feeling of being watched, but couldn't prove anything, so I shook my head. "I don't think so."

Tommy snorted. "What difference would that make? It's not like they don't know where you live."

Herb stopped short. "True, but we can never be too careful."

Tommy pointed up. "It's also daytime."

Herb thought a moment. "I guess that might afford us a little extra protection." He motioned for us to follow him. "Quick, come with me to the kitchen."

He hurried down the hall, and we followed.

My eyes immediately started to tear. There was garlic everywhere. Hung from the ceiling and the cupboards, and scattered all around the table and counters.

I waved in front of my face. "Herb, what's going on? How do you even breathe in here?"

Herb shook his head. "I'd rather be alive than breathe."

Tommy looked at me. "See?"

Herb nodded. "Yes, ever since the incident at your house, I've been vigilant. Once there's a vampire in the neighborhood it's like letting a fox in the henhouse. Especially when they know that we know. They'll do anything they can to silence us. And no vampire is getting the best of Herbert T. Dorfman, where this time, the T stands for 'taking precautions.'" Herb motioned to the table. "Sit down."

We pulled out two chairs and sat.

Herb did the same.

Tommy eyed the refrigerator. "Before we start, do you have anything to eat?"

I turned to him. "Seriously?"

He shrugged. "What? We didn't get to eat breakfast. Your mom is really bad about hosting sometimes."

Herb clapped to get our attention. "Boys, focus!"

Wendigo hopped onto the table and meowed. He was wearing a garlic collar.

Herb rubbed the cat's head. "Poor Wendigo hates it, but it's a small price to pay for safety."

I pointed to the collar. "Isn't garlic, like, really bad for animals? I mean, it could kill them, right?"

Herb nodded. "Ordinarily yes, but I needed to protect him against vampires. A rather simple spell protects him from that. Observe." He held a garlic piece out to Wendigo.

The cat tried to bite it, and the garlic disappeared from Herb's hand.

Herb smiled at us. "See? No matter how much he'd try to get a piece, he'll never be able to."

"Sweet!" Tommy yelled. "Being a warlock is awesome!"

Herb gave a slight grin. "That it is." He leaned back and pyramided his fingers in front of his face. "Now, tell me what happened."

Tommy tapped the side of his neck. "We saw two marks on Abby."

"And she was also sensitive to sunlight today," I said.

Herb winced. "That's not good. Not good at all. It definitely sounds like the initial stages of vampirism, but I'd need to see it for myself to be sure. Do your parents know?"

I shook my head. "No, I haven't told them yet."

Herb rubbed his chin. "Hmmm. We might have to, but perhaps this can be remedied without causing any panic. Parents do have a tendency to mess these types of things up. In the meantime, though, we need to make sure that she's not bitten again."

A chill shot through me, and even though I knew the answer, I asked anyway. "What happens if she's bitten again?"

Herb's eyes peered over his glasses. "She's been bitten once now, so she already has the vampire curse flowing through her. But she's not turned yet. If she's bitten a second time, though . . ."

Tommy leaned forward. "We'd have to eliminate her?"

I swatted him. "Will you stop?"

Herb shrugged. "It's a possibility, but not quite yet."

That snapped me to attention. "*What*? What do you mean, 'yet'?"

He held up three fingers. "A vampire needs three bites to turn someone."

Tommy raised his hand. "I told him that."

Herb started counting down. "After the first bite, she'll start showing some symptoms, as you've already seen. Sensitivity to light. Perhaps certain smells. After the second, she'll exhibit traits. Blending into darkness. Maybe certain cravings, such as blood."

"Blood?" My voice squeaked.

Herb nodded. "But by the third bite . . ." He shook his head. "By the third bite, it'll be too late. She'll be a full-blown member of the undead."

I gulped. "Isn't there anything that we can do?"

"Well, there is one thing," Herb said. "But it'll be dangerous."

"What?" My voice came out in a whisper.

Herb looked back and forth between me and Tommy for several moments. "The only way that I know of is to get rid of the head vampire. The one at the top of the chain. The one who sired them all. Then everyone else in their bloodline will return to normal."

I swallowed hard. "By 'get rid of,' what exactly do you mean?"

"It means," Tommy said, "that someone has to be eliminated!"

Herb nodded. "Yes."

My heart pounded. I was having trouble breathing, and all the garlic in the room sure wasn't helping.

"It's not so easy, though." Herb grabbed both ends of his necklace and pulled them back and forth around his neck. "Vampires are tough to kill, and dangerous too. On a vampire's home turf, they've probably rigged thousands of traps against intruders."

I pictured every vampire movie I'd ever seen, and realized it was not a place I wanted to get stuck inside of.

"So, what do we do?" I asked.

"Not us." He pointed at me. "You."

I patted my chest. "Me?"

Tommy leaned over and whispered. "Well, he's right. It is your sister."

"And your cousin!" I turned to Herb. "Herb, please, I need your help. You seem to know all about them. I don't know what I'm doing. I can't do this alone."

He pointed to Tommy. "You have him."

I glanced at Tommy, then looked back at Herb. "Herb, seriously, we need your help."

"Devin, I'm sorry," Herb said. "I'll help how I can, but I'm not going into the vampire house. I already told you once if there's one thing that witches and warlocks fear, it's vampires. They're immune to our magic. We'd be as scary to them as cousin Marilyn is to the rest of the Munsters."

"What?" I asked.

"All I'm saying," Herb said, "is that it's better to do it now. The longer that vampire blood is mingling with Abby's the harder it'll be to turn her back."

My shoulders slumped. "So I have to get into their house? And do what, exactly?"

"If you ever want Abby to return to normal . . ." Herb slid his glasses up the bridge of his nose. "You have to get rid of Lily's dad."

CHAPTER EIGHT

ABBY, QUEEN OF DARKNESS

The rest of the day went by in kind of a blur. All I could think about was whether I really would be able to kill a vampire. I couldn't concentrate on anything else but that. I mean, I didn't even like killing bugs because the crunching sound made me squeamish. How was I supposed to do anything to something that looked human?

"Devin!" Mom snapped her fingers in front of my face.

I looked up to see her standing over me. "What?"

She put her hands on her hips. "I've been talking to you." She pointed to my plate. "You haven't even touched your dessert. I made the apple pie especially for you. Everyone else is finished and you're still sitting there. Are you okay?"

I looked around the table and realized the only other one there was Tommy.

He held up his empty plate. "I finished mine, Aunt Megan. And it was delicious."

Mom smiled. "Thank you, Tommy."

I rolled my eyes and pushed the plate across the table. "I'm sorry, Mom. I'm just not that hungry."

Her brow furrowed. "What's wrong?"

Okay, I had to admit, there was a big part of me that *really* wanted to blurt out that our neighbors might be vampires, and how Abby was only a bite or two away from becoming a bloodsucking little monster. But I was torn. While I did want to say it, I also knew how insane it sounded. This time, I better wait for more proof. "Yeah, Mom. I was just thinking about some things."

She grinned. "I bet I know what."

"You do?" I asked.

"Yep. I'm willing to bet that you're thinking about a certain dance with a certain pretty neighbor?"

I looked at Tommy. He shrugged.

Stupid. He was no help whatsoever.

I turned back to Mom. "Well, not exactly what you think. I've been thinking that maybe it's not such a great idea for me to go to the dance."

"What are you talking about? Of course you're going to the dance!"

"I'm just saying, how much do we really know about

79

them? I mean, what if they're a psycho family of serial killers?"

"*What*?" she said. "Where do you come up with these things?" Her eyes narrowed. "Did your dad let you watch scary movies again?"

"No, I didn't watch any scary movies. But really, we don't know anything about them. Maybe they go around from town to town, putting on shows so they could kill people? The show is just there to lure them in. Did you ever think of that?"

She stared at me for a moment before speaking. "Devin, he's the principal of a school. There are heavy background checks on anyone who works in a school, so they can't be psychos."

"You haven't met some of our teachers," Tommy muttered.

"Wait, I know what this is about." Mom reached out touched my cheek. "Is this because it's your first dance? It's okay to be nervous."

"*What?* No! I'm not nervous! I just don't want to go!"

She frowned. "But you already told her yes."

"I don't care, I'm not going." As soon as the words left my mouth, I wanted to do everything to take them back, but it was too late. They were out there. They seemed to hover for a moment before landing in Mom's ears.

Her expression changed. Her nostrils flared. "What did you say?" Each word was slow, deliberate.

Tommy raised his hand. "He said he wasn't going to the dance."

"Shut up, Tommy," I said through the side of my mouth.

Mom wagged her finger at me. "Now, you listen to me. You are going to that dance, and do you know why you're going?"

I sighed. "Because I told her I would."

"Yes, because you told her you would. I understand that you're nervous, but do you know how difficult it is for a girl to work up the nerve to ask a boy to a dance? Why, when I was your age, I never would've been able to do that. So you're not going to embarrass or humiliate me, or that sweet girl, by agreeing to go and then turning her down afterwards." She turned to Tommy. "I hope you're not the same way, Tommy."

He shook his head. "No, I told him it was a bad idea, Aunt Megan."

I sighed again.

"Good for you, Tommy," Mom said, and turned back to me. "Now, there'll be no more talk about canceling." She pointed to me. "You're going. Do you understand?"

I resigned myself to the fact that I was going to the dance and nodded.

"Good. Now, go get your sister and tell her it's time to come in."

A cold wave washed over me. I noticed my hand tremble. "Come in? Come in from where?"

Mom hitched her thumb over her shoulder. "She's sitting on the porch playing with her dolls."

"*On the porch?*" I yelled and looked out the window. It was already dark outside. "Why'd you let her go outside?"

"What are you talking about? Why can't she go outside? She's right in front of the house."

"She shouldn't be outside, like, ever!"

"What—"

I didn't wait for her to finish the sentence. I bolted out of my seat, ran to the front door, yanked it open, and jumped out onto the porch.

It was mostly dark, except for a small circle of light from the overhead bulb. There was nobody there, except for Abby's doll, which was sitting propped up against the wall of the house, staring at me.

My heart pounded. I could almost hear it in the quiet of the night.

"Abby?" I called out quietly. "Abby?"

No answer.

I walked slowly toward the doll.

"Abby, this isn't funny. Come out!"

My legs trembled.

There was some rustling coming from the bushes on the side of the porch.

It was cool outside, but somehow sweat slid down my face.

"Abby, I know that you're in there. So come out now, and stop playing games!" I reached the railing and inched forward, leaning over the side. "Abby?"

A tap on my back. "What?"

I screamed and whirled around, tripping over my feet, and crashed to the porch floor.

I was flat on my back, staring up at the top of the porch.

Abby's face came into view. She stared down at me. "Did I scare you?"

The sounds of my panting echoed.

"What's the matter with you? Don't sneak up on me like that!" I took a deep breath to regain my composure. "Where were you?"

She pointed to the opposite end of the porch. "I was right over there. You looked the wrong way." She smiled. Her teeth flashed in the darkness.

I peered around her to see the other end of the porch. The only thing there was Dad's rocking chair, which creaked back and forth. "There's no way you were over there. I looked."

She nodded. "Yes, I was." Another grin. It was different than her usual ones. It was threatening. "You must've missed me. I was right over there, standing in the shadows. I like the shadows." Her voice was almost like a whisper, yet I could hear it clearly.

"Uh-huh." Okay, that did it. I never thought there'd be a way for her to get any creepier, but she found it. "Well, Mom says to come inside."

She closed her eyes and took a deep breath. "Ask her if we can stay out a few more minutes."

"No! No more being outside. Let's get into the house now! It's nighttime already."

Abby's head swiveled slowly in my direction. "I know. And I love the night."

I briefly wondered how many other kids were terrified of their little sisters. "Mom said now, so let's go!" I started to pull myself up when a shadow crossed the path of the light.

"Awww." A girl's voice. "Can't you let her stay out for just another couple of minutes?"

I whirled to the other side and fell again.

Standing on the steps of the porch was Lily. She smiled down at me. "Having trouble with your feet?"

She was wearing a T-shirt and jeans. All black. If she hadn't been so pale, I'm sure she could've disappeared into the night.

"Where'd you come from?" I asked, and scooted back across the porch toward the door.

Lily took another step and blocked my path. She leaned down. "I'm sorry if I scared you."

Abby nodded. "He gets scared easily."

"Shut up, Abby!"

Lily pointed in the direction she had come from. "I just walked up. I guess you didn't see me because you were so busy with your sister."

I scooted back some more and peeked at the door. I wondered how close I needed to be to reach it before she could kill me.

Instead, she plopped herself down beside me and smiled. "It's really nice out. I love the nighttime."

"Me too," Abby said.

I ping-ponged my eyes back and forth between them, wondering who scared me more. I motioned toward the door. "I should probably get going. I just came out to get Abby, and if I'm not back inside in a couple of seconds, everyone will worry about me and maybe call the police."

Lily laughed, like she knew I was lying. "They'd call the police for you being on the porch for a few seconds?"

I nodded. "My mom is very overprotective."

Abby shook her head. "He's lying."

"Shut up, Abby!"

Abby leaned into the doorway. "Mom, Devin wants to know if he can stay outside with his girlfriend?"

I winced, and realized that now it didn't matter if Lily was a vampire. I wanted to die anyway.

"Oh, that's so cute," Mom called from inside.

Please make this stop!

"Okay," Mom continued. "Tell him he can stay out a little longer."

Abby smirked. "You're welcome, Devin."

Mom shouted. "You come inside, though!"

Abby stomped her foot. "But I don't want to go inside yet!"

"Abby!"

She frowned. "Fine!" She turned to me and glared. "I'll wait for you inside, Devin." She stormed into the house.

I watched her go in, and the weirdest thing happened. For the first time in my life, I think I would've much rather had Abby stay with me than leave me alone.

I turned back around and jumped. Lily was closer than she was before.

"I guess it's just us now," she said.

Normally, that sentence would've been a great one, but now it just made me nervous. I eyed the door once more. "Uh, yeah, but not really. I mean, everyone is just right inside that door, and they'd hear if I screamed or anything."

Okay, yeah, I heard how stupid *that* sounded.

She laughed again. "Scream? Why would you scream?"

"Uh. I wouldn't. I'm just joking."

"Oh, that's funny." She smiled.

Wow, were her teeth bright.

"Anyway," she said. "I just came by to say hi and talk about the dance a little, if it's okay with you?"

"Oh, yeah. About the dance . . ."

"I'm really excited about it. You're going to have such a great time. I'll take you on a tour, show you around the school, and after, we're planning a really big surprise for everyone who comes."

"A surprise?" My voice caught in my throat. "Like, what kind of a surprise?"

Her eyes twinkled. "Well, that would spoil it, wouldn't it?"

The whole time I was talking to her, I found it difficult to concentrate. I kept watching every move she made. Her fingers, in case they turned into claws. Her teeth, in case they became fangs. No matter what it was, I was going to be ready.

"Devin?"

"Yeah?"

"Can I tell you something?"

This was it. She was going to confess, right before she killed me. Tell me that she needed my blood in order to survive. Or turn me into a zombie overlord, to help her rule over her army of the undead, and—

Okay, I needed to calm down.

"Uh, sure."

"I'm glad we met. It's always tough to move into a

new neighborhood and make friends, but you're really nice."

All right. I hadn't expected that.

Her eyes were really sparkling.

I was getting lost in them.

I realized that I wanted to be there for her. Be her friend. Go to the dance with her.

"I'm happy too, Lily. I'm sorry I was acting so strange."

She laughed. "Yeah, I've never seen anyone so nervous. What was all that about?" She looked me over. Her eyes widened. "Oh, I know."

I tensed up. "You do?"

She nodded. "You don't know how to dance, do you?"

I exhaled. "Yeah, that was it."

She reached for me.

I flinched. Okay, maybe I let out a squeak too, but I'm not really sure.

She laughed loudly this time. "I don't bite. Now, my dad on the other hand . . ."

"*What?*"

"Will you relax? I'm just joking!"

"Oh." I exhaled.

She reached out again, and this time put her hand on my shoulder.

Her touch calmed me. It was like a soothing feeling went through my body, like I was lying in a warm bed, wrapped in a thick blanket.

Her smile broadened.

Wow, seriously, her teeth were bright.

"Devin, you don't have to be nervous. A lot of people don't know how to dance. It's just moving to the music. A step here, a step there." She snapped her fingers. "You know what? Let me show you." She jumped to her feet and reached for me.

I held my hand up. "No, really—"

Before I could make a move, she grabbed my wrist and yanked me to my feet in one swoop.

It was like I weighed nothing at all.

I stared down at her hand as I rubbed my wrist. "How'd you do that?"

She winked. "I'm a lot stronger than I look. Remember, you never want to mess with me."

I shook my head fast. "Uh, I won't."

"Good." She placed her hands on my arms to guide me. "Now, consider this your first dance lesson. Just follow along."

"But there's no music."

She reached up and pressed her finger to my forehead. "It's all in here."

The second she made contact, thousands of images flashed through my mind. All of them, of her . . . and me.

I stared into her eyes.

They were dark and piercing. It felt like she could see everything I was thinking.

I took in every detail about her.

Her face, her eyes, her lips. Everything was perfect. But her smile was different. It was the best of all. And her teeth. I couldn't take my eyes off of them. They were unbelievably bright.

She moved to an imaginary tune, which for some reason seemed to match the rhythm in my mind.

She pointed at me. "Now, your turn."

I didn't want to, but felt my body moving along. I copied what she was doing.

She clapped. "Look at you! You're dancing."

I glanced down at my feet. It was like everything was moving on its own. Like I had no control.

Her smile got wider. "That's it. You're doing great. Just let it take you over."

She leaned closer. Her face was inches from mine when suddenly, her eyes narrowed. She backed up and looked past me. "What's that?"

I snapped out of my trance and turned to see a hand sticking out of the door. A hand carrying a cross and waving it back and forth.

I knew that hand. "Tommy?"

Tommy peered out, just sticking out his face. "Oh, hey . . ."

"What are you doing?" I asked.

"Um, just checking the weather."

Lily stayed behind me. "With a cross?"

"Uh, well, it's not really a cross. It's kind of a double-edged thermometer. Tells you the temperature and precipitation levels. I think we're expecting rain."

Lily nodded slowly. "That sounds interesting."

"Yeah, it is. Do you want to see it?" He thrust his arm out toward us, but stayed mostly inside the house.

Lily backed up another step. "I don't see any place to read temperature on it. Are you sure that's a thermometer?"

"Huh?" Tommy pulled the cross back and turned it over in his hands. "Oh. I guess it isn't working. Must be broken." He tossed it into the house, where it clanged loudly.

"What was that?" Mom called from inside.

Lily rested her hand on my arm. Jolts shot through me. "Well, I'd better go. It's getting late. Why don't you come over tomorrow night and we can continue?" She glanced at Tommy. "And you can bring your cousin."

Tommy nodded. "We'll be there."

I whipped my head in his direction. "What?"

She smiled again. "Don't tell me that you're still nervous? C'mon, Devin, I won't take no for an answer. Pretend your life depends on it."

Tommy glanced at me.

Lily laughed. "What's with you two? I'm joking!" She shook her head. "I swear, boys are so silly sometimes." She gave a wave. "See you tomorrow, Devin!"

She walked off down the path and crossed the street to her house.

Tommy stepped out onto the porch and stood next to me. "You're welcome. I think I just saved your life."

I lifted my arm to my nose and smelled her perfume still on me. My stomach churned. "Do you really think she's a vampire?"

"What are you talking about? Of course she's a vampire. You saw the way she backed up when she saw the cross."

"Because you scared her. It had nothing to do with the cross." I turned to him. "And why would you come out with a cross anyway?"

"Just in case she was about to attack you. I didn't have time to get a stake. Don't worry, though, we'll figure something out before we go there tomorrow."

"Before we go there? But I don't want to go there!"

"Why wouldn't you want to go there if you didn't think she was a vampire?"

I thought about the dancing and how it felt like I was in a trance, but maybe it was just the moment. She was so pretty, and her perfume was dizzying. Still, though . . .

Tommy swatted my chest. "C'mon! She just gave us the perfect opportunity. We'll go there tomorrow night, like she said, and if she's not a vampire then it won't hurt at all, right?"

"But what if she is?"

He flashed a smile. It was menacing. "Then we'll have a few surprises for her."

"Surprises? What surprises?"

He shrugged. "I don't know. I haven't figured that part out yet."

I groaned. This did *not* make me feel better. "I had a feeling you were going to say that."

"C'mon," he said. "Let's go in." He stepped into the house.

I was about to step in when I heard more rustling from the hedges.

I wasn't taking any chances. I jumped into the house, slamming the door behind me.

CHAPTER NINE

THE GARLIC CONUNDRUM

I lay in bed for what seemed like forever. I was exhausted from all the worrying I had been doing, but no matter what I tried, sleep just wouldn't come.

To be fair, though, my room was reeking of garlic.

Actually, most of the house did now.

Tommy had gone around to whatever windows he could reach and either dropped cloves or sprinkled garlic powder on them.

Mom wasn't happy with either the smell, or the waste, and let me know about it.

The problem was that every time she wiped it away, Tommy went back later to sprinkle some more on.

I played stupid when asked, but I also had no idea how long I was going to be able to keep this up. According to Tommy, we had to keep going until I left home for college. I tried to ignore him, but in the back of my mind I had this nagging feeling that he was right, and I *hated* when he was right.

Actually, what I hated even more was the fact that he was snoring away, peacefully, while I had a bad case of vampire-fear-and-garlic-fume induced insomnia.

I turned to stare out the window. Clouds blocked most of the moon, giving the night a foggy, ghostlike appearance. White vapors danced in and out of the branches of the tree outside my window, like skeleton fingers reaching through the leaves.

I shuddered.

This whole thing was getting to me. And as much as the signs pointed to Lily being a vampire, there was just something about her that made me think I was wrong. It wasn't just that she was so pretty, although that probably had something to do with it. It was also that she was really sweet, friendly, and funny. I mean, you just don't think of vampires as having a great sense of humor.

No, if there was any girl who could be a vampire, I don't think it'd be her. It'd probably be someone meaner. Scarier. Someone creepy. Someone more like—

"Hello, Devin."

I jumped at the sound of the voice and grabbed my pillow, holding it in front of me like a shield.

I turned to see Abby standing near the foot of my bed. I hadn't even heard her walk in.

"Abby!" I said. "What are you doing in my room?"

She smiled. "I couldn't sleep."

My jaw dropped, and my eyes widened. I zoomed in on her teeth.

No, not her teeth.

Her fangs.

They were razor sharp points. They looked like two stalactites hanging from a cave ceiling.

My hands trembled.

The pillow shook.

I did the only thing I could think of.

I screamed.

"MOM! MOM! MOM! MOM! MOM!"

Tommy sprang up. "*What's going on?*"

"She's got fangs!" I yelled.

Tommy wriggled, trying to break free from his sleeping bag but looking like a butterfly squirming out of its cocoon.

I heard footsteps crashing down the hall.

Abby cocked her head. "What's wrong, Devin? Are you scared?"

The door rattled.

"Devin?" Dad's voice. "What's going on? Why is your door locked?"

I turned to Abby.

Her eyes narrowed. "I'm hungry, Devin."

Okay, I'm not going to lie. There was definitely a shriek.

Oddly enough, though, that wasn't even the most embarrassing part.

No, that was probably saved for a few moments later when Mom used her key to unlock the door and threw it open.

She and Dad burst in.

I can't even begin to guess what was going through their minds, but they barged in to find Tommy backed against the dresser, using his index fingers as a cross, and me standing on my bed holding the pillow above my head, ready to throw it at Abby.

Yeah, I'm not sure what I was hoping to accomplish by that either, but at the time it seemed better than nothing.

Dad's eyes darted back and forth between all of us. *"What is going on in here?"*

I pointed at Abby. "She's a vampire!"

Dad groaned. "Not again."

"What?" Mom said. "Why are you talking about vampires?" She turned to Dad. "Did you let them watch scary movies?"

Dad's face fell and he shook his head. "No! I didn't. I promise."

I ran behind Mom and peered out, still pointing at

Abby. "She's a vampire. You have to listen to me. I'm telling you the truth!"

Tommy made a "T" with his hands. "Time out!"

Everyone turned toward him.

He pointed to us. "Can I please get over there, because if she vamps out right now there's nothing between her and me and I don't like my odds." He hugged the wall and moved sideways across the room, until he hopped on my bed and made his way over to us.

Mom threw her hands up. "Has everyone lost their minds? What is going on?"

I pointed again. "It's Abby! She's a vampire. I didn't want to tell you before, but she is!"

Tommy nodded. "It's true. She was bitten by the neighbors and turned."

"Yes," I said. "Look at her teeth!"

Abby laughed. "My teeth?" She reached into her mouth. "You mean these?" She opened her hand and a set of plastic vampire teeth rested on her palm.

Dad sighed. "Abby, please stop scaring your older brother."

"No, those weren't it. She had real teeth. Real fangs. I know what I saw."

Dad walked over to her. "Abby, open your mouth." He moved his hand toward her.

I reached out. "Dad, no!"

He held his index finger to his lips. "Shhh. Devin,

relax. It's okay." He cupped Abby's chin. "Now, Abby, please open your mouth."

Abby looked up at him. Her eyes twinkled. "Like I'm at the dentist?"

Dad smiled and nodded. "Yes, exactly like that."

"Okay, Daddy." She opened her mouth wide. "Aaaah."

Dad peered in. "Devin, do you want to come over here?"

I looked at Abby.

She peeked at me through the corner of her eyes.

I shook my head. "No, I'm okay over here."

Mom nudged me. "Stop being ridiculous. Go on over."

"I'll go get a stake," Tommy muttered.

I turned to Mom. "I'm not going over there. No matter what you say."

Mom grabbed my hand. "Oh, for—" She dragged me over to Dad and Abby.

Dad put his finger right by Abby's mouth.

I winced and tried picturing just what I would do when Abby sank her fangs into Dad's arm, then turned into a bat, attacked the rest of us, and—

Okay, maybe I was getting a little carried away.

Dad motioned with his head. "C'mon, Devin, just take a quick peek."

I leaned over a little, while still holding my spot behind Mom. "*What?*"

Her teeth were normal. No fangs.

Suddenly, Abby growled and lunged at me.

I shrieked and jumped back, tripping over my feet, and crashed to the floor.

Abby, Mom, and Dad burst out laughing.

Dad reached out. He was still laughing. "Devin, do you see how silly this is? Do you really believe that your sister is a vampire?"

I began to doubt myself. Did I really see fangs? Maybe I imagined the whole thing? My nerves were definitely frazzled enough to have had that happen.

I turned back to Dad. "I don't know. I guess not. Maybe I just had a nightmare."

Mom waved her hand in front of her nose. "I can understand why, with the way this room stinks. Is this why my garlic is all over the house? I want this room cleaned first thing in the morning. And no more garlic! Anywhere!"

"Okay," I muttered.

Mom leaned down and kissed the top of my head. "I really think we need to put a stop to scary movies for a while. You're letting your imagination get the better of you."

I looked down and nodded. I had no idea what to even say.

She touched my cheek. "Good. Now, get some sleep." She turned to Tommy. "And, by the way, no scary movies for you either. Your mom would kill me if she knew you were watching them."

He nodded. "I'm sorry, Aunt Megan. I told Devin it was a bad idea. We won't do it again."

I glared at him, but he wasn't paying attention.

"Great," Dad said. "Now, can we all get back to sleep?"

They all walked toward the door.

After a few feet Abby stopped, turned, and waved. "Good night, Devin. Sweet dreams." She laughed and they all walked out, with Mom shutting the door behind them.

Tommy rushed over and locked it. "Okay, we'll give it about an hour, wait until they're all asleep, and then we sneak into Abby's room, and . . ." He made a hammering motion. "Now, what do you have that we can use as a stake?"

I pushed him away. "Will you cut it out? We're not staking her."

"So what do you suggest?" Tommy pointed toward the door. "She has fangs now! How does she have fangs now?"

I shrugged. "Maybe I imagined it. It might've been those plastic teeth. It was dark, and I couldn't see so well."

Tommy waved his arms in front of him. "Maybe they were plastic, and maybe they weren't. We can't take a chance. But the only way that she could have fangs is if she was bitten for a second time, and when was she alone for that to happen?" His jaw dropped.

I'm pretty sure mine did too.

We stared at each other for a moment.

"She *was* alone," I whispered.

He snapped his fingers. "She was outside tonight." He walked over to the window and pointed across the street. "She was outside tonight with *your* girlfriend."

My heart pounded. I hated him at that moment, but he was right. I walked over next to him. "But Lily wasn't there when I got out. She only came after."

He jabbed his finger against my chest. "Or that's what she wanted you to think." He stared out. "Vampires are sneaky. Remember that." He tapped his head. "They're smarter than regular humans. They know how to manipulate feelings. What they do is, they take a simple guy like you and make you think you're special." He held up his hand. "No offense."

"Again, why should I be offended at that?"

He ignored me. "But they take him, and do what they want. You're like putty in their hands. Someone like you wouldn't stand a chance against a vampire."

"*And you would?*"

He shrugged. "Well, you have to admit I'm a little bit more knowledgeable in dark magic than you are." He put his hand on my shoulder. "But don't worry, you're lucky that I'm on your side."

"Oh, brother," I muttered.

"Now, the way I see it is that once we get rid of Mr. Moroi the curse over Abby will break. Tonight, when we go, we have to ask the right questions. Then we take care of them, and by take care of, I mean . . ." He slid his finger across his throat.

I grabbed his arm. "Stop that already! I know what you meant. I'm just saying, I don't think it's Lily. She's too sweet."

Tommy snorted. "You're so gullible."

I thought a moment. "I don't get it, though. If Abby really has vampire traits, like you said, how did she even get in here with all the garlic you put by the door?"

He scratched his head. "Good point!" He raced for the door and looked down.

All the powder had been wiped away.

"Did you wipe it away?" he asked.

I shook my head. "No! I promise."

"Well, someone did." His brow furrowed. "That's not good. I wonder if she's immune still, since she hasn't fully turned. It doesn't matter. Either way, we're going to have to be careful." He turned off my lights. "Don't worry. Tonight we're going to find out exactly what's going on and take care of it." He swatted my chest. "C'mon, let's get some sleep." He headed toward my bed. "How about you get the sleeping bag for a little? My back hurts from the floor." He didn't wait for an answer and hopped into my bed, pulling the covers over him. "Good night."

I sighed, then walked over to the sleeping bag and scooted in.

There was no way I was going to be able to sleep that night, so I guess it didn't really matter.

I replayed all the events of the day, still wondering if Lily and her dad were really vampires. Then it struck me. I realized that if they weren't, then that just might be even scarier, since I had no idea who else could've done that to Abby.

I lay there for a few moments, glanced out the window, and froze.

Was it my imagination, or were there two eyes staring back at me in the tree outside?

CHAPTER TEN

INTO THE DEN

As Tommy and I walked up the path to Lily's house, I thought about how different it was from Herb's. Herb's house still gave me the creeps. It was scary, dark, and threatening.

If anything, Lily's home seemed *overly* sweet and inviting.

Even in the dark of the night it didn't seem so bad, since the lights in front of her house gave off a calming, warm glow. There were even tiny lights planted in the ground, highlighting the flowers, which were scattered everywhere in their yard. And it also might've just been my imagination, but for some reason, it smelled like chocolate chip cookies.

I inhaled deeply. "I think I want to live here."

Tommy shook his head. "Don't you read fairy tales? That's the exact same trick witches use to lure little kids into their homes. Then they capture them to fatten them up for dinner. This is a trap, I just know it. I bet you ten dollars that we don't make it out of here alive."

"What kind of a stupid bet is that? How would I pay you if we were killed?"

Tommy thought a second. "You'll owe it to me."

"But we'll be dead!"

"Yeah, but at least then I'll have the satisfaction of knowing that I was right and you were wrong."

"You're a moron."

"I'd rather be a moron than a vampire appetizer."

"Well, you'll probably be both. And besides, you're the one who said we should come."

"I know." He tapped the side of his head. "Do you really think I'd come here unprepared? I took precautions."

"Oh, no. What did you do?"

"Don't worry. Just follow my lead." He knocked on the door.

I grabbed his shirt. "I hate when you do that! You don't tell me things and then I have to rely on you."

"I can't tell you everything because it has to be a surprise. And no offense, but you're not good at keeping secrets."

"What? I am not bad about keeping secrets! I'm better than you are."

He snorted. "If you were better than me then you would know it and I wouldn't."

The door opened.

Tommy and I turned to see Lily standing there.

She smiled. "You guys were just talking about secrets?" She looked both ways and leaned in. "Do you want to know my secret?"

Tommy and I glanced at each other.

Lily winked at me. "I'm kidding. I don't have any secrets." She laughed. "I wish I did, though. I'd love to have something about me that was really cool, that nobody else knew about."

"I bet you could think of something," Tommy said.

I ignored him. "Uh, like what kind of secrets?"

She shrugged. "I don't know. Just something that people would be shocked to learn about me. You know what I mean?"

I shook my head slowly.

She stared at me. "I bet you have some cool secrets, Devin."

My heart flipped just from hearing her say my name.

Every time I saw her I had that same reaction. There was no way she was a vampire. I didn't care what Tommy said. She was too pretty. Too sweet.

"You heard us from inside?" I asked.

She tapped her ear. "I have excellent hearing."

"I think it's called echolocation," Tommy muttered.

I ignored him. "We were just talking about something at school. It's not important."

She frowned. "Too bad. I was hoping it was something good. Anyway, I'm so happy that you guys are here." She stepped back and opened the door wider. "Come on in!"

Tommy turned his body so that he was walking sideways, facing her the entire time.

Only after a few steps did I realize that I had done the same thing.

Lily laughed. "What's with you two? You look so nervous. Is it because my dad's an actor?"

"Acting human," Tommy muttered.

"Shut up," I whispered.

As we crossed the doorway into her house, a chill shot through me. I don't know if it was my imagination or not, but I shivered.

Lily shut the door and turned to face us. Her eyes narrowed. "Well, now it's too late. You can't leave."

I gasped.

Tommy fished something out of his pocket and thrust out his arm. It was a pack of gum. He looked at it, and then back at Lily. "Uh, want a piece?"

Lily shook her head and laughed. "You guys are too much. I was just joking. Anyway, c'mon into the other room." She motioned for us to follow.

I leaned over to Tommy and whispered. "Gum? What were you going to do, pop a bubble in her face?"

He waved the pack in front of me. "I carefully

unwrapped each piece and sprinkled it with holy water, and then wrapped them again!"

"Holy water? Where did you get holy water? You haven't left my house!"

"Duh, I made it myself. I looked it up."

"What are you talking about? You can't make holy water! You're not a priest!"

He sighed. "Don't you think I thought of that beforehand? I took an online course."

"What? You can't take an online course for that!"

"Well, my certification says differently."

"You're an idiot."

"I'm taking precautions. Something that you should be thankful for."

"Just put the gum away and stop embarrassing me."

Lily turned back to look at us. "What are you guys talking about?"

"Uh, nothing," I said. "Just about the gum. I like other flavors more."

Lily shrugged. "I'm not much of a gum chewer." She turned back around.

"Now, put it away!" I said out the side of my mouth.

Tommy shoved it back into his pocket. "Fine! But don't blame me when she turns into a bat and we have nothing to protect ourselves with."

Lily continued down the hallway and into a small room with a long black leather couch. Even though there were a couple of overhead lights the room wasn't that bright, leaving several patches of darkness. Opposite the couch was a huge brown desk, with a calendar and several books on it.

I wandered over to take a look.

From what I could see, the books were all about acting. On the calendar were several marks, but there was one red circle that stood out from the rest. It was around Friday's date and in it was written one word. DANCE.

Behind the desk was an oversized chair. Actually, it was so big that it looked more like a throne. And behind the chair a bookcase which took up the whole wall. I didn't think it was possible for anyone to own that many books.

Lily sat on the couch and patted the seat beside her. "Come sit. My dad will be in any second."

I glanced at Tommy. He again turned sideways and inched his way to the opposite end, never taking his eyes off Lily, and sat down. I stood still and stared at the spot next to Lily.

She patted the couch again. "C'mon, Devin. I won't bite . . . much." She laughed.

Tommy reached for his pocket.

I pointed at him. "Stop!"

Lily looked at Tommy. "Stop what?"

Before I could answer, Lily's dad walked into the room. His hair was slicked back. He was wearing a pink button-down shirt and blue pants. "Sorry to keep you all waiting." He extended his hand. "How are you, Devin?"

I eyed it without moving. It just lingered there for a few moments.

His brow furrowed. "You don't shake hands?"

"He's nervous," Lily said. "He's never been in an actor's house before."

He laughed and grasped my shoulder instead. "Nothing to be nervous about. I'm not even such a famous actor anymore. My roles have gotten smaller and smaller over the years. But you know what they say about small parts, right?"

"They're easier to digest?" Tommy muttered.

Mr. Moroi laughed again. "I'll have to remember that. Now, just relax. Actors are just like anybody else." He motioned toward the couch. "Sit down." He went behind his desk and sat in his chair.

I eyed him a moment before I finally went over and sat next to Lily.

Tommy leaned over and whispered. "I'll get the cross ready."

"Shut up," I whispered back.

Mr. Moroi reached under his desk.

I tensed and eyed the door.

He came up with two bottles of water.

I exhaled.

He held out the bottles toward us. "Drinks?"

"Uh, sure," I said.

He tossed one each to Tommy and me.

I looked at Lily. "You don't want any?"

She held her hand up. "I drank a lot earlier. I'm not thirsty right now."

I eyed the bottle. It looked normal. I shook it slightly, not sure what I was expecting to happen. When nothing did, I twisted open the cap and took a sip.

Mr. Moroi leaned forward, placing his elbows on his desk. "So," he said. "Just curious. How long have you known that we're vampires?"

I spit water across the room.

Tommy held up the pack of gum.

Mr. Moroi eyed it.

Tommy glanced at it and swallowed hard. "Uh, piece?"

I grabbed his arm and shoved it down. "Uh . . ." My voice squeaked. "I'm sorry, what did you say?"

Mr. Moroi's expression changed. Turned serious. "I think you heard me, Devin. How long have you known that we're vampires?"

Lily reached across the desk. "Dad, stop scaring them."

It suddenly occurred to me that I had been so busy staring at Mr. Moroi I had completely forgotten that Lily was sitting right next to me.

I slowly turned toward her.

She looked into my eyes. "Devin, don't be scared."

I stared at her teeth.

There were fangs there.

I screamed, jumped away, and fell against Tommy, sending both of us falling off the side of the couch and crashing onto the floor.

"Let's get outta here!" Tommy yelled.

I scrambled to my feet and lunged for the door.

Suddenly Lily appeared in front of me, blocking the way. "Devin, wait!"

I peeked back over my shoulder to the couch to see that she was no longer there. "How'd you do that?"

She held up her hands. "Relax. Nobody's going to hurt you."

Tommy reached out again, but this time he held the cross instead of the gum. Lily recoiled and hissed, blocking her eyes. Her fangs were fully out now. My shoulders sagged. My heart pounded. We were going to die.

"Stop!" Mr. Moroi yelled.

Everyone turned toward him.

He walked over in front of Lily and eyed the cross. He also had fangs. His were larger. They looked like two daggers protruding from his mouth.

Tommy held the cross out in front of him. "Let us out of here!"

Lily turned to me but kept her distance. "Devin, I was trying to say that nobody is going to hurt you. We're just trying to keep ourselves safe."

I had no idea what to do, but when I stared into her eyes, there was a sad, pleading look to them. I needed to help her. I grabbed Tommy's wrist and pulled it down.

Tommy whipped his head in my direction. "What are you doing?"

"Let's hear what they have to say," I said.

"Are you nuts?" Tommy said. "You can't reason with a vampire!"

I glared at Tommy. "I want to hear what they have to say!"

Tommy's head dropped. "I hope you know what you're doing."

Mr. Moroi nodded at me. "Thank you." He pointed to the couch. "Please sit. If you want to leave afterwards nobody's going to stop you. I give you my word."

I looked at Tommy.

He puffed out a breath of air and closed his fist around the cross. "Fine, but if she kills us, you owe me ten dollars."

"Thank you," Mr. Moroi said, and went back behind the desk.

Lily followed.

The doorway was now clear. We could've run out, and possibly made it, but I kept peeking over at Lily.

Every time that I did, her eyes met mine. It was like her stare went through me. Everything inside me calmed down. I walked back to the couch.

Tommy didn't follow.

He stood by the door. "I'm just going to stay right over here. But you guys go ahead and talk."

Mr. Moroi smiled. "Long ago, we would have killed you for discovering our secret, but times have changed. I've changed . . . mostly. I give you my word that nobody will hurt you. I promise. But we still have to keep our existence a secret. There's a lot of hatred against vampires." He glanced at Lily. "We should know."

"Is it maybe because you guys kill people?" Tommy said.

Mr. Moroi shook his head slowly. "I used to. But not every vampire does that anymore. There are good and bad vampires, just like there are good and bad people. You can't stereotype."

"I wasn't," I said. "But I don't get it. If it's such a big secret, then why did you tell us?"

"Because you're nice, Devin," Lily said. Her voice was soft. Sweet. Calming. "There's something different about you. I told my dad that we could trust you."

Mr. Moroi nodded. "If anyone finds out about us, they'll come after us. There's a big stigma against vampires."

I ignored him. "So why did you invite us to this dance?"

Mr. Moroi laughed. "The dance is real. We really operate a performing arts school. We're trying to get new students. That's all it is. Even vampires have to earn a living."

Lily started walking toward me. "I really do hope you'll still come. It'll be fun. We're going to do a huge performance to try and get people to join the school. Who knows, you might even like it and want to join."

"Wait!" Tommy said. "Is everyone a vampire in your school?" Tommy asked.

She shook her head. "Not everyone. It's all kids who are aspiring actors. You'd be amazed at how good some of them are. Dad's a really good teacher. Like he said, he's been on Broadway, in movies, you name it."

I sat there, trying to take everything in. My head was spinning. But there was one thing I kept coming back to. "Then why did you bite Abby?"

Mr. Moroi turned to Lily. "Bite Abby?"

She shook her head. "I would never bite your sister."

Mr. Moroi turned back to me. "None of us bit Abby."

A cold feeling washed over me. "But Abby's been bitten. She had marks on her neck. She also has fangs."

Lily's mouth parted slightly. "Devin, it wasn't us. I promise."

Mr. Moroi frowned. "That means someone's gone rogue."

Those were not the words I wanted to hear. "Gone rogue? What does that mean?"

Mr. Moroi stood and started pacing the room. "It means that normally, anyone who goes to my schools does not attack people. We're trying this out for a while. Trying to live peacefully with humans." He glanced at Lily. "Granted, some of us had an easier time of it than others."

She nodded.

"Maybe Bryce?" he asked. "He can be kind of a hothead."

Lily shrugged. "I don't know."

Mr. Moroi leaned forward. His eyes narrowed. "I hope Delia's not involved in this."

Lily shook her head, looking away. "No. Delia didn't do it."

"You sure?" he asked.

She nodded slowly. "Yes."

He stared at her a moment and turned back to me. "Bottom line is we don't want trouble, and having people getting suspicious about us is trouble. Once someone discovers we're vampires, it's never good. We either have to take care of the situation or move. We don't want to move anymore, but people can be obtuse. They only know what they see in movies. They don't understand that vampires can be good as well." He turned to Lily. "I can't tell you how many times we've had to go through this."

Lily looked sad. "I'd really like to just stay in one place already."

Mr. Moroi walked over and sat on the edge of his desk closest to us. "We move for our safety. But this wasn't us. So if someone has indeed bitten your sister, then that means they've done this on their own."

"Someone from your school?" I asked.

"I'm not sure, but I think so. Especially if it's against you and your family. They must've seen Lily getting close. This might be more against us than you." He pointed at her. "To put her in a bad light. Maybe make you go after her."

"So what can we do?" I asked. "What about Abby?"

"Let me think," he said. "There's got to be a way to flush out whoever it is. And then we can save your sister."

"Wait a second," Tommy said. "I thought the only way to turn Abby back is to eliminate the vampire who bit her."

Mr. Moroi remained silent for a moment, then exhaled. "We'd prefer not to go that route. There are other ways, but we'll need both of them in the same place at the same time. Abby and whoever it was who bit her."

"What?" I yelled. "So, now I have to go to the dance *and bring Abby?*"

He nodded. "That's the only way."

"And then what?" I said. "How will we find the vampire who bit her?"

He stared at me. His eyes were cold. Unblinking. "You leave that to me."

I backed away. I realized then that there was no way that I wanted to be on the wrong side of this man. "But what do I do about Abby in the meantime?"

Mr. Moroi thought for a moment. "How many times has she been bitten?"

I held up two fingers. "Twice. But maybe it was once. I'm not really sure."

He took a deep breath and closed his eyes. "I'm sorry. That isn't good."

"What about my parents?" I said. "Should I tell them?"

Lily put her hand on mine. "Devin, that's up to you. But we're really counting on you to keep our secret, and sometimes parents aren't as understanding as kids. It's like once they become adults, they lose it. And I'd do *anything* to keep my clan safe."

"We can trust my parents," I said.

Tommy snorted. "What? You saw how they were with the Cuddle Bunnies."

Lily cocked her head. "Cuddle Bunnies? Wait a second." She snapped her fingers. "That was you? I read about that. You're a hero."

Tommy raised his hand. "Uh, it was me too."

She nodded. "Yes, both of you." She squeezed my hand. "I'd love to hear all about that one day."

I stared into her eyes. Already my fear had started to go away. "I'll tell you another time." I turned back to Tommy. "So, what do you want to do? I think we need to get an adult's help."

Tommy smiled. "I got it. I know just the person. This way, we don't have to say anything to your parents yet and still have an adult's help. Plus, he already knows you're vampires and won't say a word."

"Oh, no." I groaned. "Not—"

Tommy nodded. "Yep, Herb!"

Lily clapped. "That's a great idea! Ask him to chaperone the dance. We already asked him once, but he never answered."

Lily and Tommy continued discussing the dance but I couldn't concentrate. One thing kept going through my mind. If it wasn't Lily or her dad who bit Abby, then who was it?

CHAPTER ELEVEN

A TALK AMONG THE HEDGES

I could barely concentrate the whole walk back from Lily's house.

First off, there was that same constant sensation of being followed. It seemed to be every time I went anywhere now. But every time I turned back there was nothing there. My mind must have been playing tricks on me, and I didn't like it.

Another thing that I hated, and it might've even been worse, was that Tommy was right. Again. Which he made sure to remind me about. Again. He had said that Lily and her dad were vampires and now they had admitted it.

I guess in the back of my mind I always knew, but I kept hoping we would be wrong. I mean, who really believes that vampires are real, anyway? And to be honest, that's what was really bothering me more than anything.

I'd never really had a lot of interaction with girls before. Not that I didn't have crushes on a couple, but never anything serious. Nothing more than a couple of nods in the hallway. Maybe a meeting of the eyes from across a room. But never actual conversation with actual words.

So it was kind of a bummer that when it finally did happen, she was a full-blown member of the undead. I wasn't really sure what I was going to tell Mom and Dad about that. They didn't even like when I hung out with kids who got bad grades. I could just imagine what they might say about a girl who might bite someone's neck and drink their blood.

The other thing bothering me was if what Lily and her dad had said was true? That meant that there were others like them. And from the sound of it, probably many. Even worse, it sounded like not all of them were as nice as Lily was.

So now the main problem was that there was a vampire—*or vampires*—out there who were going to hurt us just to get back at her for something. The question was, who?

Even more important, why us?

This was horrible, since I was already afraid of being home with Abby, and now I was scared to go out as well.

And if all this wasn't bad enough, it was made even worse by Tommy's nonstop talking.

He was going on and on, and as always it didn't seem to matter to him whether I was listening or not.

"How bad would it be to be married to a vampire?" he asked.

"Nobody said anything about marrying."

He stopped in front of my porch and, as usual, ignored me. "Would she sleep in a coffin? Where would you sleep? Would you each have your own? Because there's really only room for one in there. It'd be really claustrophobic."

"Where do you come up with this stuff?"

"If you're going to be in a relationship with a vampire, I think you need to start thinking about this." He paused a moment. "Or maybe she'd make you sleep upside down, like bats. You're going to get a lot of headaches."

"Okay, enough. We don't even know if Lily likes me that way."

He snorted. "No, she just admits that she's a vampire to some guy she doesn't care about. She trusts you because she likes you!"

"Pssst . . ." someone whispered.

Tommy and I stared at each other.

"Was that you?" I asked.

He shook his head. "No, I thought it was you."

The leaves of the hedges rustled.

Tommy and I jumped. One of the hedges started to rise. My body tensed. I held my breath and thought about running, but my legs felt like jelly. The hedge kept rising until, finally, I saw what it was and exhaled.

"Herb?" Tommy and I said at the same time.

Herb was standing before us, dressed in camouflage. He had mud plastered to his face and leaves attached to an army helmet.

The only clean thing on his face were his glasses.

"Why are you dressed like that?" I asked.

"Quick, get in here!" He grabbed Tommy and me by the shirts and yanked us into the hedges with him.

I pulled his arm away. "What are you doing?"

He pried the hedges open a little and peered out. "Were you followed?"

Tommy looked out too. "What's going on?"

Herb stared out a moment longer and then turned back to us. "When you boys told me that you were going into the vampire's den, I stayed around, right outside their house, just in case anything happened. I ran back here when I saw you coming out. But if I heard any screams I was going in to rescue you."

I pointed to the leaves on his head. "How? With poison ivy?"

"No, with this!" He reached into his pocket and pulled out a bag of sand.

Tommy and I glanced at each other.

I poked at the bag. "Sand? Between that and the bottled Florida sunshine you gave us, were you hoping the vampires would enjoy a day at the beach?"

Herb frowned. "Vampires are obsessive. When items such as small, grainy things are scattered before them they have a need to count them."

Tommy snapped his fingers. "Like that little dude on Sesame Street!"

Herb nodded. "Exactly!"

Tommy pumped his fist. "I knew that stuff was real."

I sighed. "That was a Muppet!"

Tommy rolled his eyes. "Don't you think that these shows do research? They can't use it if it's not true. The last thing they need is to get sued."

"Sued by who?" I asked. "A vampire? Do vampires even have lawyers?"

"Yes," Herb said. "But you can't tell them apart." He frowned. "Sorry, this is not the time for jokes. Sometimes my quick wit just gets the best of me, and I think I'm Rodney Dangerfield."

"Who?" I asked.

He waved his hands. "Never mind now. There'll be plenty of time for me to regale you with my comedic musings later, but right now I need to know what happened in there."

I took a deep breath. "They admitted to being vampires."

Herb clenched his fist and grunted. "I knew it! We must dispose of them immediately."

"Wait!" I said. "She said it wasn't her. That she didn't bite Abby."

"And her father?" Herb asked.

Tommy shook his head. "They said neither of them did it. They blamed someone in the school."

Herb's eyes narrowed. "Like who?"

"I don't know," Tommy said. "They said it could be someone who had something against Lily or her dad."

Herb rubbed his chin. "Hmmm, a school full of actors." He nodded. "Okay, I could see pettiness there. Perhaps some would-be starlet who wasn't getting the best roles since Lily was the principal's daughter. Or maybe an unrequited love, like Cyrano for Roxanne."

I glanced at Tommy.

He shrugged.

"Yes," Herb said. "If there's one thing a theater school would be full of, it's drama." He thrust his finger up into the air. "But we will get to the bottom of this, or my name isn't Herbert T. Dorfman, where this time the T stands for 'truth-seeker.'"

I raised my hand. "Um, excuse me? I don't have any idea what you're talking about."

Herb wiped some of the mud away from his eyes. "I've decided that I'm going to help you with your vampire problem."

It was amazing to me that just a couple of days ago, I never would've believed that I'd be grateful for Herb's company, but now it was a huge relief. "Really?"

"Yessirree, Bob." Herb tapped my nose.

Okay, I was already starting to regret it.

"I was thinking it over," Herb said. "And I realized that I couldn't leave you to face this without me. Why, we're practically family."

I scrunched up my face. "We are?"

"Of course," Herb said. "We've broken bread together and I don't take that lightly. We're going to get to the bottom of this. Between the three of us, we'll be the most popular trio since the halcyon days of Earth, Wind & Fire."

"I have no idea what that means."

"It means," Herb said, "that we are going to make some beautiful music together."

Tommy peered back through the hedges. "It's funny you decided that, because they said to ask you to come to the dance also." He turned to Herb. "As a chaperone or something."

Herb arched an eyebrow. "They asked that the other night, too. There must be a reason why they're still pushing for it."

"Because they need a chaperone?" I said.

"No! Because it's a trap!"

I shook my head. "No, they're good. They told me

that there were good and bad vampires, just like there are good and bad people."

Herb turned to Tommy. "And what do you think?"

Tommy gave a half-shrug. "I don't know. She seems okay, but I don't trust vampires."

Herb nodded. "I agree."

Uh-oh. I didn't like the sound of that. Herb was flaky, and I had no time for him to keep changing his mind. I needed to reel him back in. "Wait," I said. "It wasn't like that. If anything, we're the ones who kind of brought it up. She's really nice, I promise."

"For a vampire," Tommy added.

"Hmmm." Herb paced the small area. "That might change things."

"No!" I said. "Why does it change things? There's no need to change anything."

Herb looked at us. "Vampires are capable of planting ideas, and you'd swear they were your own. They pick up thoughts in mortals and know how to manipulate them. It's one of their powers."

Tommy gasped. "I knew that too!"

I rolled my eyes. "No, you didn't."

He slapped his forehead. "So stupid of me. They manipulated us!"

I grabbed his arm. "No, they didn't! Think about it. They could've done anything to us inside that house. But they didn't. They even told us that they're vampires and let us go. Why would they do that? They're trusting us."

Herb took his glasses off and cleaned them on his camouflage jacket, before placing them back and sliding them up the bridge of his nose. "Unless that's what they wanted you to think."

"You didn't see them. They were putting their safety in our hands." I turned to Tommy. "And you saw Lily's face. She was shocked when I told her that Abby was bitten."

Tommy remained silent for a moment. "Yeah, she was. But you have to remember she *is* an actress."

I hated him. "You can totally tell if someone's acting or not."

Tommy shook his head. "Not with vampires, you can't. They're sneaky. I bet Lily and her dad are the sneakiest of the sneaky."

"Not Lily," I said. "She's telling us the truth."

Tommy put his hand on my shoulder. "Did I ever tell you about Billy Thompson?"

I groaned. "Oh, not him again. You're talking about the kid you made up?"

Again, he ignored me. "Let's agree to disagree about that. But anyway, Billy Thompson used to live in the area. Right around here, as a matter of fact."

"You already told me this," I said.

"I didn't tell you all of it," Tommy said. "And besides, Herb didn't hear."

Herb nodded. "Tell me."

Tommy continued. "Anyway, Billy went on living his life, bothering nobody, until one day he fell in love with a vampire."

"None of this is true," I said.

He went on. "So anyway, one day after a date, he comes home and he's totally changed. Like in a trance or something. His family tried to talk to him, but do you know what happened?"

I sighed. "Knowing you and your stories, I'm going to guess that he attacked everyone."

Tommy jabbed his finger at me. "Yes! Slaughtered every single one. And once word got out, the townspeople had to storm the house, because obviously, you can't let a vampire run around town. But . . ." He held up his finger. "When they got inside, he turned into a bat, flew out a window, and was never heard from again. Do you want that to happen to you?"

I pointed at him. "Last time you told me that his mother staked him!"

He raised his chin. "It was at different times."

"*How does that make any sense?*"

Herb stared at Lily's house but spoke to us. "Boys, no arguing now! We must be vigilant. We can't take anything at face value. Maybe she's telling the truth. Maybe she's not. Either way, we need to keep our guard up until we know for sure. The only thing we *do* know, for real, is that the answer will be at that dance in two nights."

"So you're definitely going to chaperone it?" I asked.

Herb thought a moment, and then nodded. "Yes. I have decided to go." He grabbed my shoulder. "But we must take precautions."

"I told you," Tommy said.

That was all I needed. Herb taking precautions, too.

Herb continued, "If we're going to take care of a vampire, we have to make sure that we do it right the first time. Because the last thing we want to do is get on the wrong side of one. If there's one thing you need to remember, it's that supernatural creatures do *not* like to be crossed. If they are, they never forget. Ever. They're like evil, vengeful elephants. No matter how long it takes, they'll try to get even." He flipped his hand dismissively. "But don't worry about that now. Let's just concentrate on Friday."

The front door opened.

Herb ducked.

Mom stepped out and looked down at us. "Why are you two standing in the hedges?"

I glanced down at the pile of leaves where Herb was hiding. "Uh, we thought we saw something."

She took a step closer. "What is it?"

"A bat," Tommy said.

Mom stepped back. "A bat? Really? Get out of those hedges right now!"

Tommy jumped out. "I said it was a bad idea, Aunt Megan."

She patted him on the head. "I wish he listened to you more, Tommy. Now, let's get inside. I want to hear all about your talk with the Morois." They went in.

I walked up the steps and turned around. "Goodnight, Herb."

"Goodnight, Devin." Herb's voice came from the hedges. "Tomorrow, we plan."

CHAPTER TWELVE

LILY UP TO BAT

It had been over an hour since I shut off the light and hit my bed, but unfortunately, the results had been pretty much the same as every other night that week.

I couldn't sleep.

Also, the same as every other night, Tommy was snoring away. I wasn't sure what it would take to actually stress him out enough to lose sleep. Knowing him, it would be something like not having enough bread for a sandwich.

The only good thing was the comfort of knowing it was only two more nights until the dance, and four more nights until Tommy's parents came home from their cruise. I wasn't sure what I was more excited about.

No, that wasn't true. As much as I hated to admit it, there was no way I would've even considered going to that dance without Tommy. He always made me braver about things. Heck, right then I was even happy that Herb was going to be there too.

The two of them always seemed so sure about magic and supernatural creatures, and I felt like the odd one out. Herb was probably already used to that stuff, being a warlock and all. But even Tommy acted like it was an everyday thing. I guess, living in Gravesend, it was.

Even though I trusted Lily, it wasn't exactly comforting to know that I was heading into a place that would be filled with vampires. Even ones who were actors. And if that weren't bad enough, the thought of having to bring Abby with me made things a hundred times worse.

But the thing I kept coming back to was that I still wasn't exactly sure what we had to do to get her to turn back into a normal kid. Well, normal for Abby, anyway.

The problem was that even if we did find out which vampire turned her, what was I going to do about it? I couldn't exactly tell the DJ to please stop the music for a minute so I could quickly kill a vampire to save my sister.

I knew Mr. Moroi said that he would take care of it. But could I really trust him?

I was hoping that Tommy or Herb would come up with an alternate plan to save Abby, but I had no idea what it might be.

What I did know was that I couldn't take much more of this. My nerves were absolutely shot.

But at least I didn't have that garlic smell in my room anymore. Tommy used the last of it around Abby's room, just in case. So far I hadn't heard a peep coming from there, but that didn't mean she wasn't up to something. Still, I felt safer knowing we took precautions, because if that meant keeping a scary little vampire away from me then I was all for it.

Now, the only vampire I had to concern myself about was—

"Hi, Devin." A whisper in the dark.

I jumped up. "Who's there?"

A giggle.

Lily stepped out of the shadows and into a beam of moonlight.

I took several deep breaths to steady myself.

"Did I scare you? I'm sorry."

My heart was pounding. "How'd you get in here?"

She smiled. "I figured now that you know I'm a vampire I could come by and visit. Thought maybe I could show you some of our cool tricks."

I eyed the door. "Do any of these tricks involve drinking my blood?"

She laughed. "You're really scared of me, aren't you?"

"No!" I thought a moment. "Should I be?"

She laughed again. "You're so funny. Do you know that after your mom invited us in once I could've gotten in anytime I wanted?" She paused a moment. "But I didn't. You can trust me."

"But you're inside now."

"True, but I thought we're friends now." She raised an eyebrow. "Aren't we?"

I stared at her for a few seconds, and realized that I hadn't answered. "Uh, yeah. I mean, yes! Of course we are." I glanced at the window. "But how'd you get in?"

She also looked at the window. "You want to know if I flew in?"

I was afraid to hear the answer, but asked anyway. "Did you?"

She smiled wide. There were no fangs. "You're asking if I turned into a bat?" She shook her head. "No. I mean, I can, but that's not how I got in." She grabbed my hand. "Do you want to see?"

Her touch was soft. Warm. "What are you going to do?"

She looked into my eyes. "Trust me." It came out more like a command than a request.

"I do."

She smiled, only this time the fangs were out.

I tried to pull my hand back. "Uh, maybe this isn't—"

It was too late.

Little by little, a foggy mist started to surround us. My body tingled. A lot. It started at my feet and worked its way up. Everything felt like when I slept on my arm and the blood slowly started circulating again. The fog grew thicker and thicker. There was a musty smell. Soon, it was everywhere. I couldn't see anything else in my room.

"Relax, Devin." Lily's voice cut through the haze. But I couldn't tell what direction it was coming from.

Through it all, though, I felt her grip on my hand. She didn't let go.

I couldn't tell how long it lasted but soon everything started to clear.

I blinked a couple of times to let my eyes adjust.

The cool air hit me. Finally, everything came back into focus, and I saw . . . stars?

I looked around and saw all the rooftops and trees of the neighborhood.

I clutched Lily's arm. "Where are we?"

"Don't you recognize the area?" Lily asked. "We're on your roof."

I glanced down and saw my feet planted on two shingles on the sloped part of my house.

I tried to scramble up, but my feet gave out from under me.

Before I could fall, Lily yanked me up.

"Careful," she said.

I squeezed her arm tighter. *"How'd you do that?"*

"I told you. Vampires have a whole bunch of cool tricks." She sat and motioned for me to do the same.

137

I slowly inched downward, trying to keep my balance. It didn't help matters that I kept peeking down to see how high up we were. Finally, I managed to ease myself down next to her. I could swear my heartbeat was echoing through the night. I stared out across a sea of rooftops. Nearby was the top of the tree outside my window. "I've never been up here before."

She looked out over the town. "Isn't it beautiful?"

I took another peek down. "Is this safe?"

"When you're with me, you are. Don't worry, I won't let anything happen to you."

A breeze blew across our faces.

Lily reached up and swiped the hair from her eyes. I stared into them. They were dark. I could feel myself getting lost in them. She smiled and squeezed my hand. A jolt of warmth shot through me.

"Am I what you thought a vampire would be like?" she asked.

"To be honest, I never really thought about it. I didn't think you guys were real."

"We're real. Actually, there are a lot of us. Not what you see in the movies, right?"

"No." I thought a moment. "But someone did bite Abby."

Lily frowned. "I'm not saying that all vampires are good. There are definitely bad ones too. Trust me, there are a few in my school. And if you think mean girls are bad in regular schools, wait until you see mean girl vampires."

"Do you think one of them could've bitten Abby?"

She shrugged. "I don't know. I guess it's possible. There are a couple who don't like me."

"Why wouldn't they like you?"

"I'm the principal's daughter. There's always going to be resentment with that. What bothers me, though, if someone bit your sister that means they've been spying on me. Because how else would they even know about you?"

"So what do we do?"

"We'll have to find out who did it first."

"And how are we going to do that?"

Her eyes narrowed. The corners of her lips twitched up. "You leave that to me. I'll find out who it was and make them sorry."

I realized, right then and there, that she meant it. This girl was probably capable of doing anything that she wanted to do. I also realized one other thing.

It was probably best not to get on her bad side.

I decided to lighten the mood. "How'd you do that fog thing?"

"You liked that one?" She laughed.

I loved hearing her laughter. It was like a song. "It was amazing. I've never felt anything like it. It was like my body was evaporating, and then put back together."

"That's almost exactly what it was."

"How'd you learn to do it?"

She shrugged. "It's not like we get a manual or anything. There's no vampire rulebook. It's just passed along. My dad taught me."

The breeze picked up, and the leaves of the trees started rustling.

"How did he learn?" I asked.

She turned to me. "He's been a vampire for a very long time."

Her words hit me, and I knew why. "I have to admit I was kind of curious about that."

Nearby, an owl hooted. There was some rustling in the treetop.

Again, she brushed the hair away from her face, and stared out. "My dad was bitten in the 1800s. 1889. England, actually."

"*You're English?*"

She smirked. "You seem more surprised about that than that we're vampires."

"Uh, no. It's just that you have no accent."

"You lose it after all the traveling we've done. We've moved a lot. I hate it. He was a classically trained actor, but that was ruined. Can't exactly have a famous career when you never age."

"How'd it happen?"

The moonlight hit her face. She closed her eyes and

it was like she was bathing in it. "He was on his way back from doing a show in London, one night, when he was attacked."

I leaned forward, hanging on her every word. "And?"

"He doesn't remember everything. He went into a coma for six weeks afterwards. When he came out of it, he had changed." She turned to me and looked directly into my eyes. "And here's the thing nobody tells you about, for when you first turn . . . there's a hunger. It's consuming. You must feed. You must have blood." She dabbed at her eyes. "Before we knew what was happening, Dad had turned Mom and me."

My jaw dropped. "So, you've been a vampire since the 1800s?"

"When he got back to being himself he felt awful about what he'd done, but it was too late. We were vampires."

I started doing the math in my head. "So that means you're over a hundred and forty years old."

"I look good for my age, right?" She laughed. "That's the good part. You don't age. You don't get sick." She sighed. "The bad is that I'm stuck at twelve forever. I've always got to be in school for appearances' sake. The friends you make will pass you by. You grow close to people and they get old and die. And there are the ones who once they discover you're a vampire, they either want nothing to do with you, or . . ." Her voice trailed off. "They want to kill you." She whispered and turned to me. "But not you, Devin. You didn't run from me." She squeezed my hand. "You're very comfortable around the supernatural."

"Well, I've met some before."

"The Cuddle Bunnies?"

I nodded. "Yeah, Mr. Flopsy-Ears." As soon as the words left my mouth, I heard how stupid it sounded.

She looked at me. "*What?*"

I winced. "He was their leader. An evil stuffed animal."

"And his name was Mr. Flopsy-Ears?"

"Trust me, he was a lot scarier than he sounds."

"But you beat him?"

"It wasn't easy, but yeah."

She reached over and hugged me. "My hero! You're not scared of any supernatural creatures."

The scent of her perfume was dizzying. My heart exploded into fireworks, shooting off in my chest.

She pulled back and smiled. "If I ever have an evil stuffed animal problem, or other supernatural creature, I'm calling you."

I have no idea why, since I knew she was joking, but I loved hearing her say that. I smiled. "Don't worry, I'll protect you."

Her eyes were piercing. "I know you will." She let go

of my hand and rose to her feet. "Want to see what else I can do?"

I nodded.

She held up her index finger. "Okay, give me a second." She stuck her arms out to the side and closed her eyes for a moment before levitating off the ground. She floated off the roof and hovered a few feet away.

"Wow!" I jumped up.

Instantly, I realized what a mistake that was. A loose shingle slipped out from under my feet and I lost my balance, sliding down the slope, fast, like a ski-jumper ready to launch. I hurtled down the side until I shot off the end, into the night. For a brief moment I was in midair, able to see everything around me. My house. The tree. The yard. My heart felt like it was going to lurch out of my throat. I closed my eyes and braced for the fall.

Suddenly, something yanked my wrist, plucking me out of the air.

The same tingling sensation. The same fog. The same mist.

In seconds, it started to clear, and I was back in my room.

My legs wobbled and buckled, and I collapsed onto my bed.

Lily leaned down. "Are you okay?"

I sat at the edge of the bed and pressed my feet onto

the floor, to feel the solid ground beneath me. "Let's not do that ever again."

"Awww, that's too bad. I was just about to show you how we turn into bats."

"Really?" I asked, a little too eagerly.

She winked. "Another time." She glanced at the clock on my nightstand. "Well, it's officially the next day. I better go."

"Yeah." I looked up at her. "Lily, thanks for stopping by tonight. That was awesome."

"Just wait. You haven't even begun to see all the really cool stuff vampires can do." She checked the clock again. "I better get back home before my dad finds out I'm gone. He's such a worrywart."

"Okay. Will I see you later?"

"Today will be tough. I have to help my dad get the school ready. But I'll see you at the dance tomorrow." She leaned down and paused a moment. We stared into each other's eyes. We seemed to linger there forever. Finally, she leaned forward again and kissed my cheek. "Good night, Devin."

It felt like time stopped. The room swirled for several moments until something pierced through the fog.

A snapping.

"Devin!"

More snapping.

"Devin!"

I blinked several times until a face appeared before me. An ugly face. Tommy.

He looked down at me. "What are you doing? You've been sitting there on the edge of the bed, staring. No offense, but it's kind of creepy."

"Huh?" I looked around the room. "Where's Lily?"

"Lily?" He also looked around. "Is Lily here?" He covered his mouth and whispered. "Should I get a stake?"

"What? No!"

He dropped to the ground and looked under my bed. "Where is she?"

I grabbed his arm and pulled him to his feet. "She's not here now, but she was." I pointed to the window. "We were outside. On the roof, and . . ." I could tell by his face that he didn't believe me. "I'm telling you the truth."

"Devin, you've been sitting there for like ten minutes already, just staring."

"What?" I rubbed my temples. "But it's true. I promise. She was here and she levitated and—"

Tommy's eyes widened. "She levitated?"

"Yeah, and then she turned into smoke and disappeared."

"She turned into smoke?" He inhaled deeply.

"What are you doing?" I asked.

He frowned. "I don't smell sulfur." He eyed my face.

"You know I'm starting to wonder if she was only in here." He tapped my forehead.

I swatted his hand away. "What do you mean?"

"It means that sometimes vampires can infiltrate your mind to communicate with you. Don't worry, though, I have just the thing." He rushed over to his backpack and pulled out a roll of tinfoil.

"Tinfoil? Why do you carry tinfoil?"

"You can never be too prepared in Gravesend."

I pointed to his backpack. "What else do you have in there?"

He ignored me and tore off two long sheets. He handed me one. "Here, put this on."

"Put it on where?"

He pointed. "Where else? On your head."

"I thought that was for aliens."

"It's for all supernatural creatures. It'll stop them from invading your thoughts." He folded his sheet into a hat and put it on his head. "Now do yours."

I crumpled the sheet of foil into a ball and threw it back at him. "I'm not putting it on, and you look ridiculous."

"I'm sorry, but there's no time to think about fashion where vampire safety is concerned."

"A foil hat doesn't work. It's stupid."

"Whatever you say, but I'm just warning you you're leaving yourself vulnerable to thought invasion, and that's the first step to becoming one of them." He reached out and put his hand on my shoulder. "I just want you to know that if it ever comes down to it and you're compromised . . ." He tapped his chest. "I'll be the one to stake you."

I shoved him away. "You're a moron. I'm going to sleep." I turned around to face the wall.

"Suit yourself, but I'm going to stay awake and keep guard a little."

"You do that," I muttered.

Within minutes, I heard the sounds of his breathing. He was out cold.

"Figures," I muttered.

I turned back around and stared out the window.

Everything seemed normal, and I was left wondering. Was Lily really in my room or did I dream it? Even stranger, did she contact me through my thoughts? Either way, I knew one thing.

This would be another night of not sleeping.

CHAPTER THIRTEEN

HOW TO SLAY A VAMPIRE

I blinked several times, sat up in my bed, stretched, and took a peek at the clock. Somehow I'd managed to sneak in a couple hours of sleep, but it didn't feel like it was nearly enough. I was groggy and disoriented. I had no idea if any of the things that I thought had happened the night before were real or not, but they sure felt real, and that was all I had to go on.

The sun streamed into the room, like it was reaching for me.

I hopped out of bed, stood, and bathed in the ray of light. It felt good. Energizing.

I noticed Tommy's sleeping bag was empty.

Now, where did he run off to?

I rubbed my eyes, walked to the window, and stared out across the street at Lily's house.

The usual. It was dark. The windows were tinted, and the shades were pulled down.

I stared at the house for several moments, just hoping to see if there was some sort of movement or activity, but there was nothing. I turned my attention to the tree. I had probably been right near it when I fell off the roof.

That was the moment when Lily snatched me out of the air. I still felt her hand on my wrist. If she hadn't, it would've been a nasty fall.

I followed the tree down, looking at just how high up it was, when I saw it. In the yard was one of the roof shingles!

I pressed my hands and face against the glass. "It happened!" I ran across the room and burst out into the hallway. I rushed down the steps, wanting to get to the yard. "There's a shingle!"

I slid to an abrupt stop in the living room.

Sitting on the couch watching TV were Tommy *and Herb*?

"What are you doing here?" I asked.

"Oh, there you are!" Dad's voice.

I whirled to face him. He was by the front door with Mom and Abby.

Abby was dressed in a hoodie and dark sunglasses.

"Where are you going?" I asked.

Dad rested his hand on top of Abby's head. "We're going back to the doctor."

Mom nodded. "Abby's still getting some headaches and sensitivity to sunlight. We just want to check it out."

Abby slid the sunglasses down the bridge of her nose and glared at me. "I know this is your fault, Devin!"

I took a step back and gulped.

Dad grabbed Abby's shoulder and pulled her away. "Abby, we've been over this. Stop scaring your brother."

Her nostrils flared.

"Anyway," Mom said, "Herb happened to stop by, and said he'd be more than happy to hang out here with both of you."

I forced a smile. "How lucky."

Mom glanced at her watch. "We shouldn't be more than a couple of hours. Call me if you need anything."

"What about the mall?" Dad asked. "I thought you wanted to get Devin clothes for the dance?"

Mom slapped her forehead. "You're right." She turned back to me. "Okay, we'll be more than a couple of hours." She stared at me a moment, and smiled before cupping my chin. "I can't believe that you're going to your first dance! My big boy. I'm so proud of you."

"*You're proud of him?*" Abby shrieked. "He's going to a dance. It's not like he saved anyone's life or anything."

"Yeah," I said. "I already did that, remember?"

Abby frowned. "You did *not* save my life."

"I did too!" I said.

Abby shook her head. "When?"

150

"Uh, the Cuddle Bunnies?"

She rolled her eyes. "Mr. Flopsy-Ears would never have hurt me."

I snorted. "Yeah, probably because you're the only thing scarier than an evil stuffed rabbit."

Abby stomped her foot. "Mom!"

Mom put her hands on her hips. "Devin!"

"Dad?" I turned to him for help.

Dad opened the door. "Uh, I think we should probably get going?"

Mom put her hand on Abby's back and started pushing her toward the door. "Abby, leave your brother alone. You'll have your own dances too, one day."

That reminded me. I had totally forgotten. "Wait! She can come to this one!"

Mom and Abby whipped their heads toward me. "*What?*"

I realized if I were going to do this, I needed to just push forward, because if I had actually stopped to think about needing to invite Abby to come with me, I probably would've thrown up all over the place.

I nodded. "Yeah. Lily said they're trying to get kids of all ages interested in acting."

Dad arched an eyebrow. "And you want Abby to go with you?"

I thought a moment. "Yes."

He pointed to her. "This Abby? Your sister, Abby?"

"Yes. Definitely. I've always thought Abby would be a great actress. And . . ." A wave of nausea washed over me. "And I think it'd be fun if we did it together." The bile rose up in my throat.

Dad leaned in and studied my face, looking me over for a minute before turning to Mom. "I can't tell. But I think he's telling the truth." He leaned in closer. "Or maybe only half-lying."

"No! I'm not. I promise. I just think Abby would be really good at it, and I want to help Lily, too."

"Well, I'm not going!" Abby shouted.

"Abby," Mom said.

She seriously drove me crazy. "Before you said you wanted to go to the dance!"

"That was before you invited me," she said. "Now I don't trust you."

"I *want* you to come!" I said.

She shook her head. "I'm not going anywhere with you. I don't know why you're saying it, but I can always tell when you're lying." She pointed at me. "Your nose does this little twitching thing, like a bunny."

Instinctively, I threw my hand up to cover my face. I hated her so much. "I'm not lying. And I don't do *anything* like a bunny! I just really want you to come."

Mom grabbed Abby's hand and started pulling her toward the door. "It's okay. She doesn't have to go."

Dad lifted his index finger and turned to Mom. "Or

maybe, Abby could go with Devin to the dance and see if she likes acting while you and I go to dinner, alone, *without kids*, and maybe go to that movie you wanted to see?"

Mom eyed him a moment. "*Eternal Love?*"

Dad nodded.

Mom turned to Abby. "Okay, change of plans. You're going to the dance."

Abby stomped her foot. "*What?*" She clenched her fists. "I'm going to get you for this, Devin!" Her eyes narrowed. "I promise." The room grew dark, except for a patch of glowing red surrounding her. Smoke rose from the ground. Her jaw unhinged and a forked tongue sprouted from her mouth.

Okay, that stuff wasn't true, but still, I took a step behind Dad for protection and peered out.

Mom pulled her. "Let's go, Abby."

The whole way, Abby stared back at me.

I realized after a moment that I was wringing the bottom of Dad's shirt until my knuckles turned white.

Dad yanked it away. "What are you doing?"

"Oh, sorry," I said.

Mom finally dragged Abby out.

"Okay," Dad said. "We'll be back as soon as we can." He cocked his head. "Wait. You were saying something about a shingle?"

"Yeah, there's a roof shingle in our yard."

He nodded. "Yeah, it must've come off during the storm last night."

"Storm? There was no storm."

"What are you talking about? It was pouring all night."

"It was?"

He laughed. "You must've slept through it. Doesn't matter, I'm going to fix it later. Well, maybe not today, but soon." He peeked over his shoulder. "Do me a favor, call your mom in around an hour or so and ask us to come home early. That way I don't have to go to the mall with them. Okay?"

"Uh, sure," I said.

"Good boy. All right, wish me luck and have fun watching movies. Just promise me you won't get nightmares, because otherwise your mom will never let me hear the end of it." He walked out, closing the door behind him.

I wasted no time and turned back to Tommy and Herb.

They were both scribbling in notebooks while watching a vampire movie.

"What are you doing?" I asked.

Tommy cleared a spot on the couch. "Sit down. We're studying."

I sat between them. "Studying? Studying for what?"

Tommy pointed his pencil at the screen. "What kills

vampires. We've been watching different movies and taking notes." He held up the notebook with VR FILE scrawled across the front. "So far we've got holy water, a blessed bullet, decapitation."

"Don't forget stake through the heart," Herb chimed in without taking his eyes off of the screen.

Tommy lifted his notebook. "I didn't." He tapped a spot. "I already wrote it down. That one's my favorite."

Herb trailed his pen down his notebook. "You also have sunlight. Infection of their blood from either an angel or a sasquatch."

Tommy jotted some more down. "We'll never get an angel on short notice, better to try for the sasquatch."

"Where are you going to get a sasquatch?" I asked.

He stared at me like he couldn't believe what I was saying. "How many times do I have to tell you? You live in Gravesend. The woods here are teeming with sasquatches."

"No, they're not," I said.

"Of course they are. And we don't even have to get the whole sasquatch. Just their blood. So all we have to do is run in, get some sasquatch blood, and run back out." He snapped his fingers. "Piece of cake."

I sighed. "Yeah, I can't imagine any problem with that."

"And don't forget religious artifacts," Herb said. "It's not just crosses."

Tommy jotted it in the VR File. "Good. That opens things up for us."

"Wait!" I looked back and forth between them. "What things?"

"For tomorrow night," Herb said. "We're walking into a vampire's den. We must be prepared."

I held my hands up. "Hey, we don't need to do anything. Lily's safe. She won't hurt us."

Tommy and Herb looked at me, and then at each other, before turning back to their notebooks.

"Okay," Tommy said. "So, we have to divide up our lists and decide who's responsible for what."

I jumped up and stood in front of the TV. "Didn't you guys hear me? I told you, Lily isn't going to hurt anybody."

Tommy took a deep breath and exhaled. "Okay, I didn't want to be the one to tell you this, but it's just that I'm not sure that we can trust your judgment right now. I think it's probably a little cloudy."

Herb nodded. "Vampires can bend the wills of even the most strong-minded individuals and turn them pliable."

"So imagine what they could do to you," Tommy said. "No offense."

I sighed. "But I just told you, Lily's not like that. She's trying to help."

Herb stood up and put his hand on my shoulder.

"Oh, Devin. I wish I could share your sense of naïveté, but the truth is you can never fully trust a vampire. I know when it comes to affairs of the heart, everyone believes they're destined to be together like Harry and Sally, but most romances are ill-fated, like Rick and Ilsa."

"Who?" I asked.

"All I'm saying," Herb said, "is you can never really trust anyone. Remember, every Michael has his Fredo."

I looked over at Tommy, who shrugged.

"It doesn't matter what he's saying," Tommy said. "It's the point behind it. Hopefully, nothing will happen, but just in case it does, we have to be prepared."

As much as I hated to admit it, they were right. We had no idea what the rest of the students were like. But we did know that one of them was probably the vampire who bit Abby. It was much better to be ready just in case. "Fine."

Herb clapped. "Splendid!"

I stared at Tommy's list. "What about Lily?"

Tommy's eyes remained glued to the screen. "What about her?"

I pictured all of the things on the list that might hurt her. "I mean, isn't this a little insulting to vampires?"

"Hey, we don't have time to worry about hurt feelings right now," Tommy said. He tossed the notebook on the couch and pointed to the TV.

On the screen, a vampire pounced on a woman and sank his fangs into her neck. Blood trickled down her shoulder.

Tommy glanced at me. "Do you want that to happen to you?"

"No, but—"

He held up a finger. "No buts!"

"Yeah, but it's basically telling Lily that I don't believe her and that I don't trust her. Maybe I should just tell her what's going on. What we're planning, so at least she's in on it with us."

"Nooooo!" Tommy yelled, waving his arms. "That's a terrible idea. You don't tell Lily anything. You *don't* know for sure that you can trust her."

"But it's like lying to her then."

Tommy sighed. "Herb, will you please talk some sense into him?"

Herb pointed at the TV and it clicked off.

"How'd you do that?" I asked.

He frowned, like it was a stupid question. "Warlock, Devin. These are just parlor tricks for me." His expression turned serious. "Anyhoo, I understand your quandary about lying to a girl you fancy. However, withholding the truth is not exactly the same as lying. And sometimes it is better to be safe than sorry. This way, if nothing happens, the young lady will be none the wiser. But if something does indeed happen with her, then at least we're ready for it." He looked down at me. "Do you understand?"

"Yeah," I muttered. "I guess so."

Herb gave me a little jab in the shoulder. "Splendid. Now, come. I think it's best that we ready ourselves while your parents are away. This way we don't have to stop to answer their constant questions."

"I'll get the balloons ready," Tommy said.

"Balloons?" I asked.

"Don't worry about that." Tommy grabbed the VR File, ripped off a sheet, and handed it to me. "Here, you take care of this stuff while Herb and I do the rest."

I read over the sheet. "There are only two things on it. 'Watch movies. Take notes.'"

Tommy nodded. "Yeah, you're still kind of the weak link here. No offense."

I sighed. "None taken."

Herb snapped his fingers and the TV turned back on. "I took the liberty of splicing together a 'Best Of' compilation. Although you're not quite getting the proper context for each vampire slaying, it does give you a general overview as to the best methods to use. Call it *How to Slay a Vampire 101*."

"Catchy title," Tommy said and waved for Herb to follow. "Okay, let's get moving." He pointed to me. "And you watch."

"Whatever," I muttered.

Tommy swatted Herb's chest. "Let's go."

I watched them walk off to the kitchen as I sat down on the couch.

I picked up the pen and sheet of paper.

On the screen, a group of kids were killing a vampire by smashing open windows during the daytime and letting sunlight into the room.

I sat down and did the only thing I could.

I took notes.

CHAPTER FOURTEEN

THE ROAD TO VAMPIRELAND

If there was one word I could use to describe the car ride to the dance, it would be "awful." Though "dreadful" and "uncomfortable" would probably fit also. I guess "uncomfortably, dreadfully awful" would be the best way to put it.

We were out in the middle of nowhere, and it was pitch black out. The only time we saw anything was when the car's headlights flashed the dirt road or trees.

I wasn't sure if these woods had a name, but "creepy" seemed appropriate. Or maybe "ghoulish." Whatever it was, I already felt like this had been a mistake. Every time I looked out the window, it seemed like there was something staring back at me. It almost felt like the trees were alive. Faces in the shadows, watching. The only thing keeping me calm was the thought of seeing

Lily. Although, to be honest, I was wondering why her school was so far away from everything else.

I held my iPhone up. "I'm getting no reception."

"We're pretty deep into the woods," Herb said. "I doubt there's any service."

Tommy pressed his face against the window. "This is like every horror movie I've ever seen."

"Maybe they just want their privacy?" I said. "Remember, she said they always had to worry about what regular people would do if they found out about their secret."

"Yeah," Tommy said. "But it's a theater school. What would actors need to be afraid of?"

"Bad reviews?" Herb chuckled. "Oh, Herb, you are so droll."

"They're just keeping themselves safe." I wished I felt as sure as I sounded. I could barely see the moon through the canopy of branches covering the road.

I took a deep breath. Already, it felt like air wasn't reaching my lungs. Every few moments I tugged at the tie Mom had made me put on. I hated ties. It felt like I was wearing a boa constrictor around my neck, but she insisted I have one for the dance.

I might not even make it to the vampires, if this stupid tie strangled me to death.

If that weren't bad enough, we were in Herb's weird car. He said to think of it as our limo for the night, but really, it looked more like that car that they carried dead people in. I don't think I would've even minded so much, except that Herb was playing the oldies radio station. So far the only songs I knew were ones I'd heard on TV commercials. I had no idea that they were actually really songs. I thought they were just created for the advertisement. There was nothing new, nothing modern, nothing good.

Even worse, Tommy had called shotgun, so while he was in the front, I was stuck in the back with Abby. The whole ride she had been sitting there with her arms crossed, her nostrils flaring, glaring at me. I pretended not to notice, but seriously, she was creeping me out.

"All right," Tommy said. "We need to change the station."

Herb swatted his hand away. "Don't touch that. That's Blue Oyster Cult, 'Don't Fear the Reaper.'" He hummed along for a moment. "It's a great song."

Tommy turned down the volume. "It stinks. I can't focus listening to this and we need to concentrate."

"Did you bring everything?" Herb asked.

Tommy lifted up his backpack. "Yeah, I got it all in here."

I leaned forward, trying to see inside. "How are you planning to get all that into the dance?"

Tommy shrugged. "We just carry it in. What's the big deal?"

"I don't know," I said. "Vampires are pretty smart."

"*Vampires?*" Abby shrieked. "*There are going to be vampires there?*"

I motioned for her to be quiet. "Shhh!"

"*Your girlfriend's a vampire?*"

I jumped back. "She's not my girlfriend!" I thought a moment. "And I didn't know she was a vampire! I swear!"

"I don't believe you!" She stomped her foot. "I want to go home!"

Herb peeked at us through the rearview mirror.

"Abby, listen to me," I said.

Her lips curled upward. "I said I want to go *home!*" She sprouted fangs and snarled. There was a brief moment when everything seemed to stop in time, but it didn't last long. My heart pounded. My legs trembled. She lunged at me.

I screamed, leaped for the opposite end of the car, and reached for the door handle. It wouldn't budge. "Open the door!" I screamed.

Abby grabbed my shirt and yanked me back, letting loose a low growl. I fell to the seat and stared up at her. Her eyes were red. She snarled and opened her mouth wide.

I always knew Abby would be responsible for killing me one day.

Suddenly, Herb threw something at us.

Sand!

It landed everywhere. In my eyes. In my hair. Grains were all over us and the back seat.

"What the heck?" I yelled.

Abby let go of me.

I didn't waste the opportunity. I jumped away, wiping everything off of my face and out of my hair.

Her eyes turned brown again, and she started counting each grain.

"Herb, pull over!" I yelled. *"Let me out of this car!"*

"Relax," Herb said. "There's no need to panic anymore. If we let her, she'll be busy with those grains for hours."

"Forty-three, forty-four . . ." Abby muttered.

"Show them," Herb said.

Tommy held up several bags.

"And if need be," Herb said. "I have plenty more."

Tommy nodded. "And if worst comes to worst, you mess with her count."

"What are you talking about?" I asked.

"You just interrupt her a little, and then it'll naturally take over. Watch." He turned around. "Sixteen, seventeen, eighteen . . ."

Abby continued counting. "Nineteen, twenty, twenty-one . . ."

Tommy flashed a smile. "See? What'd I tell you?"

I glanced at Abby, who was still sorting grains of

sand. "So what are we going to do if something bad happens? You don't have enough sand for everyone."

Herb shook his head. "No, it wouldn't even work on everyone. Only the closest to it. The experienced vampires would only be distracted for a little before they'd regain their composure. But sometimes, a few moments can be the difference between life and death."

Tommy wedged the extra bags of sand into his backpack. "Okay, it's pretty stuffed now. I don't think there's room for anything else."

I tried to see over the seat. "What else do you have in there?"

He pushed the bag down by his legs. "Too much to go into now. But it should keep us safe in case any rogue vampires get any ideas."

"I'll carry it in," Herb said. "Since I'm chaperoning, maybe nobody will question me, and we can hide it under a table or something."

I settled back in my seat. "I'm telling you, I don't think we'll need this. Lily's not bad."

"It's not just for Lily. She already told you that there are some jealous students. We'll be ready in case the green-eyed monster rears its ugly head." Herb slowed the car and pointed. "We're here."

I couldn't believe my eyes.

The place was huge. Two stories high and close to the length of a football field. Trees all around us in every direction. Floodlights shone on the school, making it look more like a Hollywood premiere than a local small town theater-school dance.

"A lot of people already here," Herb said. "There must be a couple of hundred cars."

"A hundred," Abby said. "One hundred and one, one hundred and two . . ."

"There's no lot here," I said. "Where do people park?"

Herb pulled into a spot on the grass. "I guess just anywhere."

"I thought everyone would fly here." Tommy flapped his hands.

Herb shut the car off, reached over, and grabbed the backpack. "Okay, everybody stay close and let me know if you see anything weird or suspicious."

Tommy turned to him. "What are you talking about? The whole place is weird and suspicious."

"Well, weirder," Herb said.

People started filing through the front doors.

I put my hand in front of Abby's eyes. That broke her out of her trance from counting.

She looked up at me. "What do you want?"

"Abby, we're going in now."

"To the vampires?" she shrieked.

"Shhh!" I motioned for her to keep quiet. She didn't seem to have any idea that she had been bitten, and I wasn't going to tell her. "Abby, I need you to keep calm. Yes, Lily is a vampire, but she's nice." I grabbed her hand. "It'll be all right, okay?"

She wrinkled her nose. "There are no nice vampires."

Tommy nodded. "For once I agree with her."

"There are," I said. "You can't just say all vampires are bad."

She crossed her arms. "Name me one good vampire."

"Uh." I looked to Tommy for help.

He shrugged. "I think she's right."

Herb looked back over his shoulder. "Well, there's Count Chocula."

Tommy snorted. "Please, do you really think that guy eats only cereal?"

I threw my hands up. "He's not real!"

"Look!" Herb pointed. "Almost everybody's already inside. We better get going."

I took a deep breath and nodded. "Okay."

Herb turned to Tommy. "Ready?"

He glanced at me. "Yeah."

Herb opened the door and looked back at all of us. "Off to Vampireland we go."

CHAPTER FIFTEEN

THE NOSFER ACADEMY OF TALENTED UNDERSTUDIES

The only thing more amazing than the outside of the school was the inside. Mom and Dad had taken us to see shows at the Gravesend Center for the Performing Arts a couple of times, but even that was nothing compared to this place.

I'm not sure how many students went to this school, but it was enormous.

The center of the building, where we had walked in, had the highest ceiling I had ever seen. A huge chandelier hung above us. Black balloons were scattered in patches on the floor. I guess they wanted us to walk through them or kick them around. There were also hundreds bunched together, taped to the walls.

It looked more like a fancy wedding than a school production.

Straight ahead was a large doorway. Above it hung a sign, which read THEATER. On either side of the doorway were two curved staircases leading up to a balcony. The lobby had a dance floor laid out in the center with a podium at the front. A DJ station with a couple of turntables was off to the right.

Around the dance floor were tables and chairs, all draped in black.

Kids were already starting to sit.

There were a lot of adults here, too. I guess chaperones or teachers.

"What do we do now?" Tommy asked.

I shrugged. "I don't know. Lily said there'd be a performance of some kind first." I glanced over at him. "Why is your jacket so bulky?"

"Don't worry about it. I have a lot of stuff under here that we need." His eyes widened.

"What's wrong?" I asked.

He pointed past me.

"You're Lily's friend, right?" a guy asked.

I turned to see three guys around my age, maybe a little older, standing in front of me. All of them were dressed in some kind of dark spandex outfits. The one in the center was taller than the others. His eyes were dark, and his hair was long. He looked like a rock star.

I nodded and stuck out my hand. "Uh, yeah. I'm Devin."

He didn't offer his.

I felt stupid, and pulled mine back.

He sneered. "I'm Bryce."

I glanced at the two guys standing next to him, but he didn't introduce them.

His expression never changed. "Lily's talked a lot about you."

Normally hearing that would've made me ecstatic, but the way he said it made me take a step back.

I felt cold. Nervous.

His eyes darted back and forth between us until they rested on Abby. He sniffed a couple of times, pointed to her, and smirked. "She looks familiar. Have I met her before?"

Abby just stared at him, without blinking, like she was in a trance.

"Abby?" I said. Nothing. I snapped my fingers in front of her face. "Abby?"

Bryce smiled. "Maybe she's just in awe of being in a theater school."

I clenched my fists, wanting to take a step toward him, but my legs buckled. I honestly had no idea what to do.

Herb stepped between us. "She just has one of those faces." He pushed me back. "Well, it was nice meeting you, but I'm sure you have to go get ready."

Bryce gave a quick laugh. "Yeah, I guess so." He eyed me once more. "Maybe we can talk more later." He started walking away and his friends followed.

Almost as soon as he left Abby came to, like nothing had ever happened. "Devin, this place stinks!" She looked up at me. "I can't wait to get home and tell Mom that you brought me to a vampire dance. You're going to get in so much trouble."

"Abby, I—"

Herb grabbed my shoulder, leaned down, and whispered in my ear, "You must not let them goad you until we know who the full cast of characters are."

"Herb, this isn't a book or a movie!" I said. "He's obviously the one who bit Abby! He acted like he already knew her, and she went into a trance."

"Maybe," Tommy said. "But remember vampires are sneaky. You can't trust them for anything."

"Devin!"

Her voice!

I turned to see Lily walking toward me. She smiled, and all the bad things that I had been thinking about just washed away. "Hey, Li—"

Before I could finish my sentence, she wrapped her arms around me and gave me an enormous hug. "I'm so glad you came."

I'm not going to lie. That hug was probably the best feeling I'd ever had.

She let go, and I wished I had a rewind button.

"Having fun?" she asked.

"Uh, we just met your friend Bryce."

She rolled her eyes. "I bet he was a jerk, wasn't he?"

"The biggest," Tommy said.

I leaned close to Lily and whispered. "I don't know, but I think he might've been the one who bit Abby."

Her brow furrowed. "Why do you say that?"

I looked back over my shoulder to see if he was near. "Just the way he was talking. It was like he had a secret he wasn't sharing, and Abby kind of went into a trance."

She glanced over at Bryce. "Okay, keep Abby close to you. After the song, I'll try to get to the bottom of it."

"Song?" I asked.

She smiled. Her teeth were so bright.

She swatted my arm. "Of course! I told you there would be a small performance first. I'm going to sing."

"You are?" I said.

Her smile grew wider. No fangs. "Well, it *is* a performing arts school." She touched my arm. "Remember, even though I'm singing to everyone, just know that I'm really singing only to you."

My heart pounded out of control.

Tommy raised his hand. "When is the food going to be served? I'm kind of hungry."

I turned to him. "Seriously?"

"What?" He shrugged. "Maybe if your mom actually

made sure we had something to eat before she went out I wouldn't be so hungry all the time."

Lily laughed. "I promise you nobody will go home hungry tonight."

"Where should I go?" Herb asked. "I want to take my chaperoning duties seriously."

Lily pointed to an area on the far end of the dance floor. "You're going to wander around with the other chaperones and get everyone seated."

Herb gave her a thumbs-up. "The Herbmeister is on it." He started to walk, but when Lily wasn't looking he turned to Tommy. He made a "V" shape with his fingers and pointed to his eyes, before pointing to Lily.

Tommy nodded.

I looked back and forth between them and mouthed, "What?"

But neither of them answered before Lily grabbed my hand. "Come!" She led me to a circular table close to a microphone stand. The table had a long green cloth draped over it, which reached the floor. Several RESERVED signs were on top of it. She pulled out a seat. "I saved these for all of you." She patted it. "You sit here, Devin."

I counted the chairs.

Five.

"Are you going to be sitting with us after?" I asked.

She squeezed my hand. "Of course." She looked past me and frowned.

I followed her gaze and saw a group of three girls nearby. All of them had dark hair, but one had red streaks in hers.

I tried to see her face, but she kept her back to us.

The three girls were standing close together. It looked like they were whispering to each other with their hands over their mouths.

"Who are they?" I asked.

Lily didn't take her eyes off of them. "The one with the red streaks is Delia. The other two are Shaylee and Maya, but they're harmless without her. We call them Delia and the Deliettes. They do whatever Delia wants."

Tommy walked up behind us. "What's their problem?"

Lily shook her head. "They don't like me. Delia's always been jealous. And the other two hate me because she tells them to."

I craned my neck to try and get a look at her face, but Delia never turned.

Something tugged at my shirt.

I looked down to see Abby.

She crossed her arms. "Can we go already? This is the worst party ever."

A tapping of the microphone echoed throughout the lobby. Everyone turned to see Lily's dad standing behind the podium. People who had been sitting rose to their feet. The room erupted into applause.

Mr. Moroi smiled and waved to the crowd. "Thank you! Thank you!" He motioned toward the tables. "Please, everyone be seated."

Lily squeezed my hand once more. "My cue to go!" She let go and took off.

"Good luck!" I yelled after her.

She stopped in her tracks and turned around. "You never wish an actor good luck!"

I winced.

Oh, no. I messed up. *Why did I have to mess up with her?*

She laughed. "Relax. I'm just joking."

I breathed a sigh of relief.

"I swear," she said. "You look like all the blood was drained from your body. Anyway, I gotta go! See you soon." She ran off again.

Everyone in the room made their way over to the tables around the dance floor to sit.

I sat between Abby and Tommy at our table.

Tommy picked up one of the RESERVED signs. "Hey, awesome!" He held it out to show me. "This one has my name on it."

I looked over and saw that all the signs had one of our names on them.

Mr. Moroi waited a moment for the crowd to settle into their seats. He looked over the room, and then snapped his fingers.

Instantly everything went dark.

Gasps around the room.

A spotlight turned on, shining on him.

He smiled. "And welcome to Nosfer Academy's First Annual Recruitment Dance!"

More applause.

Tommy turned the sign over in his hands. "This is so cool. Do you think they'll let me take this home?"

"I don't know. Now be quiet, he's talking!"

"But look at these! They're not like little cardboard things. I guess they're metal or something." He tried bending it. "This must be expensive. I bet this school has a lot of money."

"I don't care," I whispered. "Everyone's trying to listen and you're talking." I glanced at the tables around us and even through the shadows I could make out several nearby people glaring. I lifted my hand and mouthed, "Sorry."

A couple of them rolled their eyes and turned back.

Mr. Moroi paced back and forth in front of the room. "As our students know, we requested that each of you bring at least one guest to our party tonight." He looked around. "Well, I'm thrilled to announce that not only did every single person here accomplish that feat, but the majority of you even brought more than one!"

Everyone jumped to their feet, clapping.

He pointed to our table. "With my daughter, Lily, bringing four guests all by herself!"

The people around us turned to our table and clapped.

Tommy bowed slightly, raised his RESERVED sign, and waved to everyone.

Mr. Moroi motioned for everyone to sit back down. "Thank you. We'll get to our feast and dance after, but first we have some entertainment."

"LILLLEEEEEEEE!" A few guys from the back of the room shouted.

A pang shot through me. I didn't even know these guys, but I hated that they seemed to be her friends, and maybe even know her better than I did.

Mr. Moroi laughed. "Yes, yes. Lily is in it. But everyone worked hard. A lot of preparation went into tonight. And we just hope that afterwards you'll consider joining us. Because, if you don't . . ." He looked around the room. "Then I'm not sure I can let you leave."

Tommy glanced at me.

"Just kidding!" Mr. Moroi said. "But I think this performance will sell our school better than anything else."

I pictured how that girl, Delia, must've been reacting. According to Lily she was already jealous enough. I just hoped she wouldn't do anything mean to Lily.

Tommy had his hands on either end of the RESERVED

sign. "I can't even bend this." He tried again. "I wonder what it's made of."

"Will you stop with the stupid sign?" I said a little too loudly.

"Shhhh!" From all around us.

Abby around the room. "So, all of these people are vampires?"

A few heads turned toward us.

"Quiet!" I motioned for her to keep her voice down. I leaned close to Abby. "I don't think all of them."

Her eyes narrowed as she looked around the room. "I *hate* vampires. You're the worst brother ever! Next time you go to a party with monsters, go without me."

"I had to bring you!"

"Shhhh!"

"Why did you have to bring me? You never want to bring me anywhere!"

Again, my first instinct was to tell her that she had been bitten, but the last thing I needed was to have Abby panicking. "Forget it," I said. "I told you they're friendly. Nobody's going to hurt anybody."

"So, without further ado," Mr. Moroi said, "here's our show!"

Suddenly, the lights went out. Music blared from the nearby DJ's table. A spotlight went on next to me! I jumped back. Lily was right by my side! I hadn't even heard her moving. She started to sing, and it was beautiful.

I'd never heard a voice like hers. It was soothing. Haunting. It went through me. Her voice wrapped around me like a cocoon. It took me a moment to realize that I should pay attention.

"You came into my life," she sang.

Our eyes met.

"And suddenly everything is clear."

She smiled.

I couldn't feel my body move.

"Yuck!" Abby said. "This is the stupidest song ever!"

"Quiet!" I hissed.

Soon another spotlight turned on. Then another. Within moments there were several around the room.

Delia and her friends were on the opposite side of the room. Even though we were indoors, for some reason they were all wearing sunglasses. They were singing backup to Lily, and it was obvious.

There must've been around seven or eight kids singing, but none of them were as good as Lily.

They sang a couple of more songs, and then moved to the center of the dance floor for a sketch.

I barely paid attention to what was being said because I couldn't concentrate on anything but her. It was something about how great it was to be a student at the school. Some of it was funny. Some of it was stupid.

But I didn't care. Lily was amazing, funny, and confident. There was no way that I could have ever gotten up there to do what she was doing.

Then that kid Bryce showed up and made his way to the center of the floor near her. They shared the scene together as boyfriend and girlfriend.

"I wish we could always be together at this school," Bryce said.

"Maybe there's a way that we can," Lily said.

My stomach churned.

"Wow," Tommy said. "They have really great chemistry." He glanced at me and saw my frown. "But the dialogue isn't believable at all."

"Shut up, Tommy." I stared at him. "And will you put that stupid sign down?"

"This sign isn't stupid!" Abby said. "This play is. Nobody in a real school talks like that."

"It's a sketch," I whispered.

"Well, it's a stupid sketch."

Toward the end of the scene Lily caught my eye again. She winked.

I smiled back.

Bryce noticed it and glared.

I slinked back into my seat. That kid made me nervous. There was something about him. Something strange. Something dangerous. Well, besides him being a vampire.

The scene ended, and everyone in the audience jumped to their feet and applauded.

I did too.

Lily and the other actors took a bow before rushing off and through the doors to the theater.

The place stayed dark, except for a few lights around the dance floor.

A whistling sound came from the DJ's mic.

We turned toward the table.

He was dressed all in black. His head was shaved. He tapped the mic a couple of times. "Are you ready?" he screamed. Cheers erupted. The DJ smiled. "Let's dance!"

"What about the food?" Tommy said.

Music blared from the speakers. Kids flocked to the dance floor.

I looked back over my shoulder toward the theater doors for Lily, but she still wasn't out.

Unfortunately, Bryce and his friends were. Also unfortunately, he was staring right at me.

I motioned with my head. "Tommy, look!"

Tommy looked over. "Wow, I don't think that kid likes you!"

"I don't blame him," Abby muttered.

Bryce didn't turn away.

"This is so stupid," I said. "Is he actually going to start a fight with me because of Lily?"

Tommy shrugged. "Well, vampires are notoriously jealous creatures."

"And stupid," Abby said.

I swallowed hard. "What am I going to do if he comes over here to fight me?"

"Get beaten up," Abby said.

Tommy banged the RESERVED sign against the edge of the table. "Don't worry about it."

"What do you mean, 'Don't worry about it'? Do you think I could beat him?"

Tommy snorted. "Him?" He shook his head. "No way. I mean, look at that guy and then look at you. No offense."

"None taken. But what do I do if he comes over?"

Abby scowled. "Tell him that the only thing worse than this dance was his acting."

Tommy leaned over to me. "I really don't think you should say that."

I pushed him away. "I wasn't going to!"

"Good," Tommy said. "All those creative types never like to hear criticism. And you especially don't want to critique an actor who's a vampire." He ran his finger along the edge of the sign. "You know what? These sides are pretty sharp. I bet we could even use it as a weapon if we needed."

"A weapon? How do you plan on using a RESERVED sign as a weapon? Telling the vampires they're not allowed to sit here?"

He held the sign out to me. "Feel how sharp the edges are. With the right force we can use this to take one of their heads off, or at least slit their throats." He waved the sign. "Maybe we do that right now with Bryce."

I shoved the sign away. "Stop it! We're not taking anyone's heads off."

He banged the sign against the table and held it out to me again. "That guy over there isn't playing. Right now you have the element of surprise. Use it. When he comes, take it and swipe at his throat!"

"Just put it away, already!" I shoved it back toward him, accidentally jamming into his hand.

"Ow!" he yelled, and dropped the sign on the table, where it rattled from side to side for a moment until it came to a stop.

Tommy winced, clenching and unclenching his fist several times. He held up his hand.

I could see the slice across his palm. Slowly, a sliver of red spread out over it. A drop trickled down his hand to his wrist, where it fell to the table and splattered.

The music screeched to a stop.

Instantly, all talk ended and everything in the room turned silent.

Every head turned slowly toward us.

Tommy and I glanced at each other.

This wasn't good at all.

CHAPTER SIXTEEN

VAMPIRE BUFFET

There are times in your life when it almost feels like you're watching a movie, instead of living it. This was one of those times. The only problem was it was a movie where I was possibly about to be killed. Everything around me was going on in slow motion. Every head turned toward us. Every face staring.

The object of their attention was Tommy's bleeding hand. Nobody moved. It was silent . . . but only for a moment. Soon, a collective growl echoed throughout the lobby. I scanned everyone's faces. Most of them had a hunger.

I frantically searched the room, but didn't see Lily or her dad anywhere. Snarling sounds were all around us. Corners of lips lifted. Fangs sprouted from mouths.

Tommy grabbed a napkin and wrapped it around his wounded hand.

A red stain seeped through.

"Is Bryce still coming?" Tommy asked.

I grabbed his arm. "I think our problems are a whole lot worse than Bryce right now!"

Some of the kids at the next table took a couple of steps toward us.

Tommy unbuttoned his jacket. "Don't panic! I got this."

Two more steps.

I grabbed his arm. "Tommy!"

"STOP!" A voice boomed through the room.

Everyone in the room turned toward the DJ table.

The DJ stared out over the crowd, before bringing the microphone up to his mouth. "My brothers and sisters." His voice was raspy. "I do not want any of you to even think about harming any of our guests."

I exhaled and grabbed my chest. My heart was pounding out of control.

"No!" He paused a moment, and then held up a small black box with a large red button on it. "At least, not until we have some privacy." He pressed the button and suddenly, all around us, shutters slammed down outside over the windows and doors.

The music blared once more.

Oh, no.

The DJ brought the microphone back up to his mouth. "Ladies and gentlemen, enjoy your dinner!"

His eyes turned red and his fangs sprouted. His skin turned gray, his ears pointy.

I quickly scanned the room and saw that the same thing was happening to most of the crowd. There were a few snarls at first, but then they multiplied, until the sounds were everywhere.

I realized something immediately.

We were surrounded

Instantly, all around us was chaos. People screamed. Vampires swarmed guests, biting into their necks and shoulders.

At the next table blood spouted into the air, like a fountain.

I grabbed Abby's hand. "Let's get out of here!"

She screamed. "Let go of me!"

I ignored her and yanked her after me.

Tommy pointed. "To the theater!"

He was right. All around us there was pandemonium, but at least there was a clear path to the theater doors. Well, almost clear.

There was someone who stood between us and the theater. Actually, three someones.

Bryce and his friends, who had turned into the same gray creatures as the DJ had.

"What about Bryce?" I yelled.

"Follow me!" Tommy shouted. He reached into his jacket and pulled out . . . a water balloon?

I ran behind him, dragging Abby along.

Bryce and his friends blocked the path.

Tommy hurled the water balloon at them. It smashed into Bryce's face, exploding and splattering him and his friends. There was a sizzling sound, followed by a trail of smoke.

Bryce screamed and clutched at his face. His two friends scattered.

We ran past them and into the theater.

"Quick!" Tommy yelled. "Help me with the door!"

We started to shove the door closed, when a couple of other kids ran up.

One wedged his foot between the door and the frame. "Wait! Let us in, we're not vampires!"

"Nice try, bloodsucker!" Tommy said, and tried to push the door closed.

The kid looked panicked. "No, really, we're not! Let us in!"

Tommy pulled a cross from his jacket pocket and pressed it to the kid's forehead.

Nothing happened.

Tommy opened the door a little. "Okay, hurry up!"

Three kids streamed past us and into the auditorium.

"Close it!" one of them yelled.

"What about any others?" I shouted. "We can't just leave them out there!"

Suddenly, Bryce thrust his head through the

opening of the doorway. His eyes were blazing red and his fangs bared. His face was scarred from where the water balloon had struck him.

He shoved the door open some more, reached in, and grabbed Tommy's shirt.

His fingers were longer, with sharp, black nails.

He pulled Tommy to him.

Tommy struggled to break free, punching Bryce's arm.

It did nothing.

"Help!" Tommy yelled. "Do something!"

I launched myself against the door and heard a snap as it slammed closed.

"Lock it!"

We bolted it shut and leaned against the door, panting.

I glanced over, jumped back, and pointed. "Tommy!"

Still grasping Tommy's shirt was Bryce's severed arm.

Black blood dripped from the stump.

Tommy waved his arms frantically. "Get it off, get it off!"

I shook my head. "I'm not touching that thing!"

Abby huffed. "You two are such babies!" She marched over and grabbed the wrist and plucked it off. She waved the bloody end at us.

Tommy and I cringed together as we pressed against the wall.

She pointed the stump, alternating between me and Tommy. "I told you that I didn't want to come, but nobody cared! When we get home I'm so telling Mom everything!"

I couldn't take it anymore and decided to tell her. "Abby, the only reason we brought you here is because you were bitten. You might've been bitten twice, I don't know, but the only way to make sure you don't turn into a full vampire is to get rid of the one who bit you."

"I knew it! I knew there was a reason you asked me to come. I'm telling Mom and Dad." She jabbed the arm at us. "You better make sure I don't turn into a vampire, or I'll—" She tossed the arm on the floor, where it landed with a *splat.*

Black blood seeped out into a puddle, looking like an oil spill.

I stared at the arm and my stomach heaved, but nothing came out. "That is soooo gross! We chopped off his arm! *How did that happen?*"

Tommy shrugged. "Vampire bodies are soft. They're like super strong, but their bodies are still soft. If you hit 'em just right, you can even punch your way through their flesh." He pointed to the arm. "Just stay away from that thing. Blood from a freshly killed vampire is like acid. It can even burn through metal. Be careful."

Smoke rose from the black blood. There was a sizzling sound, and I watched as it ate its way into the floor.

Abby grabbed our shirts. "Who cares about the stupid arm? *You let me get bitten?* Didn't you put garlic everywhere around the house?"

Tommy nodded. "Yes, but in the morning the powder by the doorway was gone. Someone must've wiped it away."

She frowned like she didn't believe us. "Who would wipe away garlic?"

He shrugged. "I don't know. Maybe someone who wanted to hurt you or us. All I know is that it was gone."

"And outside," I said. "I think you might've been bitten there too. When I went out, I heard something in the hedges."

Tommy jabbed his finger at me. "And that's when you saw Lily."

I shook my head. "No, I told you, Lily came from the other direction!"

Tommy laughed and turned away from me. "She's a vampire! She can appear anywhere."

I clenched my fists. "There was someone else out there. I even heard it after she left."

Tommy waved dismissively. "Who else could it be? It's not like you have a thousand people stalking you."

Abby's nostrils flared. "I'm telling you right now, if I turn into a vampire, I'm attacking both of you first!"

I gulped and took a step back. "It wasn't Lily though."

Tommy stormed over and pointed toward the door.

"You know it was her! How do you explain what's going on out there? Lily invited us to be feasted on. She pretended this whole time, since she knew you were so gullible."

I heard snarls and screams coming from outside. There was scratching at the door. I shuddered to think about what was going on out there. Then it hit me. "She wasn't out there."

"What?" Tommy said.

"Lily. She wasn't out there. She's not part of this."

Tommy snorted. "Of course she's part of this."

"Her and her dad weren't out there!"

"She might not have been out there," Tommy yelled. "But she knew what was going to happen! It was a setup. She invited you to the dance knowing what would happen. You were probably her contribution. It's like a potluck. Everyone has to bring something."

"Did you say Lily?" said a voice from one of the seats.

We turned to see the three kids we had let in, two guys and a girl. They were sitting in some of the nearby seats around the theater.

The kid closest to us spoke up. He looked like he was a couple of years older. He had blood streaked on his face, and his shirt was slightly torn by his chest.

"Who are you?" Tommy asked.

"My name is David, and I'm sorry to interrupt, but you're talking about Lily? Lily Moroi?"

I nodded slowly, already knowing that I didn't like the way this was going.

David continued. "I met Lily in my drama club. She started talking to me about the school, and said she thought I might like it."

Tommy turned to me and shook his head. "The only thing worse than a vampire is a two-timing vampire."

"Shut up, Tommy," I said, but with no force behind it. I was too stunned. "Maybe it's a different Lily Moroi?"

Tommy rolled his eyes. "Yeah, there must be a thousand Lily Morois running around."

David shrugged. "She said she was the principal's daughter."

I winced.

Tommy turned to me. "I'm pretty sure your Lily is the principal's daughter, right?"

I gritted my teeth. "I heard him!"

We turned to the other two. They were both closer to my age. The guy had his head buried in his hands.

Tommy snapped his fingers. "Hey! What are your names?"

The boy lifted his head. He was sweating. He looked petrified.

I tapped Tommy's shoulder. "Take it easy with him. Look how scared he is."

Tommy whispered out the side of his mouth. "I am taking it easy, but we have to be safe and make sure."

The kid wiped his brow. "I'm Oren, and I also had a Lily invite me."

I threw my arms up. "Oh, c'mon!"

Tommy's jaw dropped. He held up three fingers.

I'm not going to lie. I wasn't sure what bothered me more, the fact that Lily might have been trying to kill me, or that she invited other guys to the dance.

Oren wiped a streak of blood away from his forehead. "Yeah, she had been helping me with math and talked about this dance. She was cute, so I thought I'd come check it out."

Another pang.

Tommy paced the room. "I'll say this for Lily, she really knows how to take advantage of lovestruck guys."

"I got it, Tommy," I said.

"Seriously," he said. "She got three different guys to fall for this?"

"I said, I got it!"

Tommy walked over to the girl. "And what about you?"

She looked back and forth between us. "I'm Kesha." She shook her head. "And I don't know any Lily. I met a Delia. She invited me. But right at the start of the dance she turned and tried to attack me."

"Yeah, almost everyone at my table turned," David said.

Oren nodded. "Mine too."

Tommy started pacing the room, looking like a detective in those old movies. "Okay, here's what we know." He counted off on his fingers. "We've been invited to be the main course at some vampire buffet. We have no idea how many are out there, but I'm going to guess over a hundred." He pointed to Abby. "We've got a little vampire-wannabe in here that we have to keep an eye on." He turned and eyed everyone. "Now, there's also the other concern."

"What's that?" I asked.

"We have to make sure that none of you were bitten."

"What are you talking about?" Oren said.

Tommy pulled the cross out. "Just what I said. I need to make sure that nobody was bitten."

David threw his arms up. "Nobody was bitten! Otherwise we'd be dead, wouldn't we?"

Tommy shook his head. "No. That's what the beginners think." He tapped his chest. "Vampire experts, like me, know the truth." He walked slowly over to David, holding the cross out in front. "You see, there are two types of vampire bites. Ones to feed and ones to turn someone. The ones to turn someone are lighter, gentler. You never know it's happening." He pointed to Abby. "Like what happened to her. But . . ." He held his index finger up. "The ones to feed are rough. Vicious. Gruesome. They really sink their fangs into you. And usually they come in swarms. When several vampires get you at once, you don't need more than one bite from a particular vamp. You're going to turn. Might take some time, but it'll happen. So now we have to be sure that none of you were bitten." His eyes narrowed. "Now, show me your necks."

Kesha and Oren tilted their heads to show Tommy.

Tommy checked them over. "Looks clean." He turned to David. "Now you."

"You already held a cross to my forehead!" David yelled.

"You might not have turned yet," Tommy said.

David reached out and grabbed the cross. "*Okay*?"

Tommy looked at it and nodded. "Okay, just making sure."

David sighed. "Instead of trying to act all tough, why don't you figure out a way to get us out of here? There are only six of us in here, and who know how many of them out there!"

"Six?" I looked around. "Wait a second. Where's Herb?"

We all turned to the door.

"Oh, no," I muttered. "We have to go get Herb!"

Tommy grabbed my arm. "We can't get Herb now! If he's out there, he's either dinner or one of them by now. We have to stay in here or figure a different way out."

David jumped out of his seat. "I vote for getting out now!"

Oren and Kesha nodded.

"I'm with him," Kesha said.

"Me too!" Abby said.

I held my hands up. "Okay, hold on! We can't go until we find out who bit Abby. That's why we're here."

David took a step down the aisle toward the stage. "I don't know, that kind of sounds more like a *'you'* problem than an 'us' problem."

"Yeah, sorry," Oren said. "I don't want to be a jerk, but I'm not messing with any vampires. I say we get out of here."

"Devin's right," Tommy said. "We can't leave yet. We have to find the right vampire."

David laughed. "You want to fight a hundred vampires with only one cross?"

Tommy smiled. "No. I want to fight vampires with these!" He opened his jacket.

It was lined with water balloons, sharpened pencils, one dart gun, one water gun, one barbecue lighter gun, several crosses, two small bottles of garlic powder, and several bags of sand and salt.

He tapped one of the bottles of garlic powder. "Mix a little of this in the water balloons and it works wonders." He smirked. "That's what I used on Bryce."

Kesha jumped out of her seat and rushed over to him. She checked out everything in Tommy's jacket. "You don't mess around."

Tommy smiled. "When you live in Gravesend you always have to be prepared."

I rolled my eyes. "I knew that would come up."

"I had more stuff." Tommy hitched his thumb over his shoulder. "But it's in Herb's bag. If we want to get out of here alive we're going to have to find it."

David pointed to the stage. "Well, there should be another way out of here, backstage. From there we can split up, if you want. You go find your vampire and the rest of us will look for a way out."

"So what are waiting for?" Kesha asked. "Let's get out of here, before they remember that we're in here." She moved toward the center aisle of the theater, which had a red carpet leading all the way down to the stage.

Tommy ran in front of her to block the path. "Wait! Let's make sure that we're all prepared. I think I've got everything covered, but just in case I missed something, what do we know that kills vampires?"

David looked over Tommy's jacket. "We know crosses."

"Actually," Tommy said. "It's any religious artifact. Vampires don't discriminate. They can be killed by any religion as long as you believe."

"Where'd you hear that?" I asked. "Was that another *Scooby-Doo*?"

He shook his head. "That was a *Dora the Explorer* Transylvania episode I watched when I was little."

I sighed. "You're making that up."

He stared at me without blinking. "You didn't watch as much TV as I did, so you don't know."

"I think I saw that one," Kesha said.

"You didn't see it!" I said. "There was no episode. He's making it up."

Tommy turned to her and shook his head. "Let's just agree to disagree with him. Now, does anyone have any other methods?"

Kesha's eyes widened. "Oh, don't forget about fire."

Tommy nodded. "Got the lighter."

As everyone called each thing out, Tommy patted them in his jacket.

"And taking off their heads," Abby said.

She seriously creeped me out.

Tommy nodded. "Yeah, but we don't have anything sharp enough. We might have to improvise."

"Silver?" Oren said.

David shook his head. "That's for werewolves."

"Actually," Tommy said, "silver works. Especially if you carve a little cross onto it." He looked around the room. "Anything else?"

"I really would like to speak to Lily first," I said. "I really don't believe she had anything to do with this."

Abby let out a loud sigh. "Are you always this dumb? She's using you until she eats you. She'll probably rip open your chest and eat your heart first chance she gets."

David pointed at her. "Yeah, I agree with the creepy little girl."

Out of nowhere, Kesha pointed past us and screamed.

We whirled around to see a trail of black blood where Bryce's severed arm had been. The trail headed in our direction until it veered off by the last row of seats.

"Where is it?" I yelled.

"I have no idea!" Tommy said. "Everybody check under the seats!"

Everyone dropped to the ground.

"I don't see it," David said.

Kesha jumped onto a seat, spinning in every direction while looking for the arm. "I'm scared. Please, let's get out of here!"

I felt a sharp pain in my leg.

I looked down and saw the hand digging its nails into my calf. I felt the wet trickle of blood seeping down my leg.

"It's on me!" I screamed.

Tommy pulled out a water gun and ran toward me, squirting it again and again. The arm sizzled, and boils popped up on its skin.

After several more shots, the hand released its grip and dropped to the floor.

David kicked it away toward the door.

"Let's get out of here," Tommy yelled.

We all huddled together as we walked down the center aisle.

Everyone kept looking in different directions, searching for anything that might pop out. The slow pace was excruciating.

Behind us the door rattled.

I squeezed Abby's hand. "They're back."

"Keep moving," Tommy said.

Now there was banging on the side doors. There were more of them.

My legs trembled.

We neared the stage, but nobody rushed toward it. We stayed huddled together in our turtle-like formation.

"Keep going," I whispered, not entirely sure to whom.

We walked toward the steps on the right side of the stage and carefully made our way up.

"Which way?" Tommy asked.

David pointed. "There should be doors leading out of here somewhere in the wings. We have to hope that they don't decide to come here before we can get out."

We crept along, inch by inch, until we neared the side curtain. Suddenly, from behind us, there was a creaking noise. We all whirled to face it. A trapdoor in the floor of the stage creaked again and flung open.

A head popped out.

CHAPTER SEVENTEEN

BATS IN THE WINGS

"Herb!" I yelled, and ran over, amazed that I was actually happy to see him.

Herb tossed out the backpack, which landed with a thud on the stage floor. He reached up. "Quick, help me out."

We plucked him from the crawl space.

He collapsed, sprawling out on the stage.

"Herb, are you okay?" I asked.

He gave a slight shake of his head and took a deep breath. "I barely made it out of there in one piece."

Tommy leaned down. "Any vampires after you?"

Herb's brow creased. "You might say that."

Tommy grabbed the dart gun from inside his jacket and pushed a pencil into it before aiming it at Herb.

Herb swatted Tommy's hand. "I'm not a vampire, but that doesn't mean it wasn't close. But like Peter Cushing squaring off against Christopher Lee, I managed to hold my own."

David, Oren, and Kesha turned to me, but I shrugged.

"How'd you get away?" I asked.

"When the DJ first stopped the music, I was on the other side of the room from you kids. And by the way, his song selection was atrocious. Not sure how you can have a dance without a single Bobby Rydell track, but that's neither here nor there."

I sighed. "Herb, can you just get back to the story?"

He sat up. "Oh, yes. Very well. Anyway, as I said, when everyone turned, I saw you make it into the theater. I was way too far away to join you, so I had to improvise. I grabbed the backpack and made my way through the school until I found the area beneath the theater, and that's how I found you."

"Were you followed?" Tommy asked.

"Well, I don't think so. But who can be sure? Anyhoo, we can't stay here forever. The bad news is we're surrounded. The good news is I know where Lily and her dad are."

The words hit me like a hammer. "Where?"

Herb pointed up. "I saw Moroi drag Lily off when everything started."

My heart lurched. "He dragged her off? She's in trouble. We have to help her."

"Oh, c'mon!" a couple of them said at the same time.

"Dude," David said. "She played us. She played all of us. She's a vampire. That's what they do."

Tommy put his hand on my shoulder. "I told you! You can never trust a vampire."

"Either way," Herb said as he got to his feet, "we must get upstairs if we hope to save Abby."

"Upstairs?" I pointed to the theater doors. "The vampire who bit Abby is out there, only we don't know which one it was."

Herb grabbed my shoulders, and turned me to face him. "Devin, you're not thinking. Even if it was one of the vampires out there who bit Abby, we can still rescue her by confronting the main vampire. Which is who?"

"Lily's dad, but—"

Herb wagged his finger in my face. "No buts." He tapped the side of my head. "Think. If Moroi is in charge of this school, then I'm willing to bet that all the vampires in here are from his line. They can all be traced back to him. Remember, the only way to remove the curse from anyone bitten is to eliminate the main vampire. So that's every student, every vampire, and—"

"Lily," I said.

Herb nodded. "If there is any humanity left in her, the only way to retrieve it is to get Mr. Moroi."

"But he's been really nice," I said.

Tommy snorted. "Obviously. I mean, only nice vampires invite someone to be eaten. He deserves what he gets."

I sighed. "Oh, I'm sure Lily will be extremely thrilled that we killed her dad."

"Or," Herb said, "she might be happy that you saved her from enduring an eternal curse."

I thought of what Lily had said to me about hating never growing older. About missing friends who passed her by. I wondered if there was some part of her who would be happy if she got to grow up like a normal girl now.

On the other hand, we still had no proof that either Lily or Mr. Moroi knew about this. I knew it looked bad, but they had left before the vampires did anything. As unlikely as it was, there was something nagging at me. There was something else that I was missing.

Abby's brow furrowed. She looked up, and then turned in a full circle.

"What's wrong?" I asked.

She stared a moment longer. "Do you hear that?"

I tried listening a moment, and shrugged. "What?"

Tommy looked around. "Wait, I hear it too."

Finally, I heard it.

It was a squeaking sound. Actually, a whole bunch of squeaking sounds.

"What is that?" I asked.

Herb slid his finger up the bridge of his nose to push up his glasses. "Bats. Those are bats."

The flapping of their wings brushed against the doors.

"Which way is it coming from?" Abby said.

I pointed to the back of the theater, where we had walked in. "From there."

Tommy shook his head. "No, it's coming from over there." He pointed to a door on the side.

Everyone looked in different directions and I realized the truth. It was coming from all sides.

There was also one other thing I realized. It was getting louder.

Oren grabbed the side of a chair. "Could we please get out of here already? I really don't feel well." He looked pale and was covered in sweat.

"What's wrong?" Kesha asked.

His eyes rolled up into his head and he collapsed to the ground, trembling and shaking.

We all rushed over, forming a huddle over him.

"What is it?" I asked.

Kesha bent down next to him and felt his forehead. "He's burning up."

Herb grabbed us and pushed us back. "I think we need to move!"

Everyone took a few steps away.

Herb pointed to a red spot on Oren's shirt by his

arm. There was another one on his side. "He's been bitten a couple of times. I bet there's also another one that we don't see! He's going to turn."

Tommy aimed his dart gun at Oren. It was loaded with a sharpened pencil. "Stand back!"

Herb shoved Tommy's arm down. "No. We can't do that to him. He's not a vampire yet."

Oren's eyes popped open. He smiled. "Oh, I don't know about that." There were fangs in his mouth. He lunged at Herb.

Tommy shot him with the pencil.

Oren shrieked and dropped like a stone to the theater floor. He writhed around trying to reach for the pencil, which was stuck in his back.

"Why isn't he dead?" Tommy screamed.

"The heart!" I yelled. "A vampire has to be staked through his heart! Even I know that!"

Before he could respond there was a loud whistle behind us.

We whirled to see Kesha standing by the theater doors.

My heart dropped.

She also smiled.

Even from here, I could see her fangs.

"You guys are so much fun," she said. "How about we also let my friends in to play?" She turned and opened the door.

CHAPTER EIGHTEEN

HOW MANY BITES DOES IT TAKE TO GET TO THE CENTER OF A WARLOCK?

The back of the theater turned black, like a flying eclipse.

What seemed like hundreds of bats swarmed in through the doors, blocking everything else.

The sounds of shrieking and wings flapping filled the theater.

"Run!" David screamed. He slid through the open trapdoor of the stage.

Herb unzipped the backpack, took out a Super Soaker, and began firing wildly at the incoming bats.

Shrieks echoed across the stage.

"When did you get a Super Soaker?" I yelled.

"When I saw how effective it was when you used it against the Cuddle Bunnies. Now move!"

I grabbed Abby.

"Let go of me!" she screamed, stretched her arms out to the sides, and closed her eyes. "I want to see the bats . . ." The last few words came out in a whisper.

"We don't have time for this!" I yanked her off her feet and scrambled for the trapdoor, sliding the last few feet until we fell into it.

Suddenly there was nothing beneath us.

We fell, but only for a second, before landing on something soft.

"Oof!" I grunted. I opened my eyes and reached down to feel below me.

We had landed on an oversized mattress.

David was nowhere to be found.

"Watch out!" Tommy said.

I looked up to see him at the trapdoor.

"Move!" he screamed and threw the backpack down, where it bounced once and came to rest on the mattress. "Now me!"

I jumped out of the way a split second before he landed.

He pointed to the ladder. "Herb's still up there!"

I ran to the ladder and jumped onto the third rung before I climbed the rest of the way up. I popped my head out to see Herb swinging the Super Soaker from side to side, firing wildly in every direction at the whirlwind of bats around him.

"Herb, c'mon!" I shouted.

Herb inched his way to the trapdoor. "Get back, Devin! I've already been bitten a couple of times. Go without me!" He inched back some more.

"What?" I yelled. *"You've been bitten?"*

"Yes, now go!"

"I'm not leaving you here, Herb!" I looked down at Tommy. "Throw me a bag of sand!"

"What?"

"The sand!"

Tommy opened his jacket, yanked a bag from his pocket, and tossed it up to me.

I caught it and ripped the bag open. "Herb, watch out!"

Herb stepped out of the way and I threw the sand across the stage.

Grains scattered in every direction.

There was one giant shriek, and the bats all flew after it.

Every single one of them transformed into human-looking beings and began to count.

"Herb, let's go!"

Herb dropped to his knees and crawled to the trapdoor.

I climbed down a few rungs to let him come through.

He placed his foot on the top rung and lowered himself through. He smiled at me. "Many thanks, Devin!"

I pointed up. "Herb, shut the door!"

His eyes widened. "Oh, yeah!"

He reached up and grabbed the latch.

Suddenly, Oren's face appeared in the opening. He glared down at us, his mouth opened wide, looking like a shark about to take a bite out of a seal. He chomped down on Herb's arm.

"Aaaaaaaaaagh!" Herb screamed.

Tommy jumped onto the ladder beside me and took aim.

A pencil whizzed past and landed with a loud thwack sound in Oren's chest.

He let loose an ear-piercing shriek and fell away.

"Darn it!" Tommy yelled. "I missed the heart."

I grabbed Herb and pulled him through. Tommy helped him down the ladder. I slammed the trapdoor closed, bolted it, and jumped back down. Tommy and I surrounded Herb. His arm had gashes from bite marks. Blood streamed everywhere, looking like a red river running down it.

I undid my tie and wrapped it around his wounds.

He winced.

"Help me knot this," I said. Tommy grabbed one end and helped me finish it off.

I studied Herb's face and saw the fear and worry in

it. I kept waiting for something to happen. Fangs to sprout. Fingers to grow. But nothing changed.

"Herb," I said. "What happens now?"

Already beads of sweat were collecting on his upper lip. "Well, now we have a problem. We either have to destroy the vampire who just bit me or the head of the bloodline, which I'm betting is Moroi, and we probably have to do it fast."

I already had a bad feeling about what he was going to say. "And what happens if we don't?"

Herb turned to us. "I've had three bites. It won't be long. It could be five minutes, an hour, several hours. There's just no way of knowing. Already, the vampire's curse is flowing through my blood. If we don't find out who it is soon I'll be deader than Barry McGuire's career after 'Eve of Destruction.'"

I glanced at Tommy.

He shrugged.

Herb slid the glasses up the bridge of his nose. "The worst part will be the hunger. I might turn on both of you. I'm telling you now—I can't live as a vampire. If that happens, I need one of you boys to promise that you'll kill me."

Tommy thrust his hand up. "Ooh, I'll do it!"

I cocked my head. "What?"

Herb gripped my shoulder. "Devin, you must not be weak here! I must know that I can count on you if it comes to it. Sentimentality has no place with vampirism."

"Hey!" Tommy said. "I already called it."

I waved my hands. "Stop talking about killing Herb!"

Tommy started to open his mouth, but I glared at him and he closed it.

I pointed toward the door. "We've got to get out there and find the vampire responsible for turning Herb and Abby, and—" I scanned the room and my heart dropped. "Where's Abby?" I bolted from the spot and searched everywhere. "She's not here! Help me find her!"

"Quick!" Tommy said. "There might be someone here. Take a dart gun."

Tommy handed me one from his jacket. We loaded them with pencils, and slowly searched the room. We looked behind beams, and in the shadows along the walls.

Nothing.

Above us there was scratching at the trapdoor. The sounds of bats screeching.

I saw movement out of the corner of my eye.

A door opening.

I whirled and fired the dart gun . . . into a metal box on the wall.

Sparks shot out.

Lights flickered on and off before finally shutting off completely.

We were in the dark.

"Nice going," Tommy said.

"I saw a door opening," I said.

"It was probably Abby leaving," Herb voice called out in the darkness. "That means she's close."

There was a buzzing sound and the lights flickered again.

"There must be a backup system trying to restore things," Herb said.

Tommy grabbed my arm and spun me around. "Look!"

Straight ahead of us, in the shadows, was a sliver of light from a partly open door.

"Abby!" I yelled.

We rushed over to it and peered out into the middle of an empty hallway, stretching in both directions.

Abby was gone.

CHAPTER NINETEEN

THE T STANDS FOR TROUBLE

Each sound I heard walking through the hallways of the theater school made me jump.

The overhead lights flashed on and off, buzzing each time they did.

Herb, Tommy, and I swiveled side to side, ready to fire. Tommy and I had the dart guns loaded with pencils while Herb held the Super Soaker filled with water mixed with garlic powder.

The lights flickering made it difficult to concentrate. Behind every shadow, I pictured a vampire lurking, ready to jump or fly out at us.

Even that wasn't as bad as the fact that we were walking with Herb, who was basically a ticking time bomb.

It wasn't easy knowing the one who was guarding

your back might soon be the one who was biting your neck.

The worst part of all was there was still no sign of Abby. I had no idea where she could've run off to and I was scared to find out. Hopefully, she hadn't turned yet. Abby with vampire powers and a hunger for blood wasn't a good mix.

And on top of everything else, there was Lily. I hadn't seen her since her performance, and had no idea what to believe. Actually, that's not true. The big problem was that I was starting to believe what everyone else was saying, and I hated that I did.

Herb took the lead, creeping along.

"Devin . . ." Someone whispered my name.

I turned toward the voice. The hall was empty. My chest heaved. The sounds of my breath were only drowned out by the buzzing of the lights.

On. Off. On. Off.

I began to wonder if I had just imagined things. I moved slowly, keeping an eye out behind us.

"Deviiiiiiiiin."

This time, it was to the side. I whirled and pointed the gun. *"Who's there?"*

I turned to see Herb and Tommy staring at me.

Tommy's brow furrowed. "Who are you talking to?"

"You didn't hear that?" I asked.

Herb shook his head slowly.

"Hear what?" Tommy asked.

I looked around again. Still nothing.

Herb motioned with his fingers. "Let's go!"

We continued down the hall. My hand was stiff from gripping the gun so tightly.

"Help me, Devin . . ."

This time, I recognized it. *Lily's voice!* My heart thumped. "Lily?"

Tommy and Herb spun around.

"Where?" Tommy hissed.

I pointed, but continued moving my hand around the hall. Finally, I dropped my arm. "I'm not sure."

"What do you mean you're not sure?" Tommy said. "Did you hear her or not?"

I nodded once, but then stopped. "I don't know."

Suddenly, the lights cut out.

"Just great," I whispered.

"Everyone stay together," Herb said.

All I could make out were shadows. "I can barely see you."

Something scurried behind us.

I spun and fired.

THWACK!

"I hit it!" I yelled.

We all stared into the darkness.

It was silent, but only for a moment

From the other direction, there were sounds.

Screeching sounds. Flapping sounds.

Herb took a step back. "I think we should—"

"RUN!" Tommy yelled.

We took off in the direction where I had fired the shot.

At that moment I didn't care what was there. It was better than facing hundreds of bats.

The overhead buzzing sound returned. The emergency lights flickered back on. Then off. On. And off.

The hallway was bathed in an eerie red glow.

"Keep going!" Herb yelled. He pointed straight ahead. "There's an exit down the hall!"

Sure enough, there was a door marked EMERGENCY EXIT ONLY in red block letters.

My chest felt like it was going to explode, but I didn't dare stop. We raced for the door. I reached it first and launched myself against it.

Clanging alarms went off, drowning out the squeals of the bats and the buzzing of the lights.

It was chaos and confusion, and my head felt like it was about to explode.

We were in a stairwell.

"C'mon!" I yelled, racing up the steps.

I didn't bother looking back to see if they were following. I yanked open the door at the next floor and rushed out.

Classroom after classroom went by, and I was

amazed at how much it seemed like a normal school. There were even signs on the hallway walls promoting school events.

I briefly wondered if there was such a thing as vampire elections and what their slogans might be. "*I promise to make this school suck*"?

The bell kept clanging away, pounding in my brain. I couldn't think straight.

At the end of the hallway, I turned a corner and tried the first door I saw. *Open!* I jumped through. Thankfully, Herb and Tommy followed. It was dark in here.

We shut the door.

"Get down!" I hissed.

We dropped to the ground, pressing our backs against the bottom of the door, making sure to stay below the door's window.

On the other side of the door, we heard the loud sounds of flapping going by.

I was too scared to even peek out. Too scared to even take a breath.

Finally, the last sounds of flapping flew by, and it was quiet.

I waited a few beats more, until I felt comfortable enough to exhale.

The sounds of our breaths broke the silence.

"How'd you know they wouldn't follow us in here?" Tommy asked.

I shrugged. "I didn't. I was only hoping. I thought maybe the bell was throwing off their radar."

"Echolocation," Tommy said.

I nodded. "Yeah, that."

Herb moved up into a crouch. "That was actually brilliant, Devin." He motioned for Tommy and me to move over. "Now, let me take a look to see where they went." He peeked out the window.

Tommy and I took a couple of steps back.

Herb pressed his face against the glass.

After a few moments, he still hadn't said anything.

Tommy and I glanced at each other.

"Uh, Herb?" I said. "Are there any vampires?"

"Well, there's one." Herb turned around.

But it wasn't really Herb anymore.

Well, it was, but this Herb now had fangs.

CHAPTER TWENTY

A WARLOCK WITH BITE

In all the years I'd spent watching horror movies, I have to say, this was the first time I'd ever seen a vampire with a comb-over.

Herb took several steps toward us. His fangs were out. His fingers had long, black nails. His smile was wide and evil. He took another step. His eyes narrowed. "I need to thank you, Devin." Another step. "You got rid of everyone else, allowing me to feed on my own."

I held my hands in front of me. "Herb! Snap out of it!" I snapped my fingers a couple of times. "You're our friend! Don't give in to it!"

"The hunger comes first. And when there's a hunger, consider me just like Lola. Whatever Herbie wants, Herbie gets."

Even when he was a vampire, I had no idea what he was talking about.

Tommy and I backpedaled, trying to push desks and chairs in his way.

Herb continued toward us, tossing them aside.

Tommy raised the dart gun.

"You can't," I said out the side of my mouth.

"You heard what he said before," Tommy said through gritted teeth. "He wanted us to kill him if he became a vampire!"

"We can change him back!"

"We'd have to get past him first!"

We kept moving until we reached the wall.

Herb laughed. "You seem to have run out of room."

Tommy pointed the dart gun at him. "Herb, I'm warning you. I will use this."

Herb snarled. His expression changed. He looked meaner. Ferocious. Ridges started forming along the bridge of his nose. His face started looking more animalistic. He grabbed the end of the last table between us and threw it across the room.

I didn't see anything left of him.

Herb lunged.

Tommy fired.

There was a loud squeal and Herb fell to the ground.

The pencil was sticking out of his side. He tried to

pull it out but it snapped in half, leaving the pointed end still stuck inside him.

"Let's go!" I shouted.

Tommy and I jumped over him but before I could make it across, Herb snatched my ankle and yanked me to the floor.

His eyes were blazing. He opened his mouth.

I grabbed the front of his shoulders and tried to push him back, but he was too strong.

His teeth kept snapping at my arms, getting closer.

Suddenly, something was thrown over his head, and he recoiled and shrieked.

I smelled it before I saw it. A garlic necklace.

Herb clutched at it, but couldn't get it off.

Little trails of smoke appeared each time it touched his chest, accompanied by a sizzling sound. Herb shrieked repeatedly, or maybe it was one continuous sound. Either way, it was awful.

Tommy grabbed my hand and yanked me away. "C'mon!"

I looked down at Herb. "What do we do about him?"

He lifted his index finger. "You're right. Get the Super Soaker!"

"Are you kidding me?"

Tommy ran over to grab the Super Soaker, then ran back to the door. "You want to save him? Then we need to go find the vampire, or vampires, who did this to him. There's nothing that we can do for him now. C'mon!"

Herb reached out for me.

Something in his eyes.

I could swear that I saw the real him through the monster.

"C'mon!" Tommy yelled again and grabbed my wrist.

"But—"

"No buts! We can't do anything for him now! Let's go!"

I took one last look at Herb and ran off after Tommy, out of the classroom.

We went out quietly into the hall and took a look around.

Thankfully the alarm had stopped, but the red glow remained.

"Where to?" I asked.

Tommy continued walking, swiveling from side to side, with the Super Soaker drawn. He looked like something out of a cop movie. "We have to find the principal's office. That'd be my bet."

"How are we going to find that? This school is enormous."

"Usually the principal's office is near the front of the school."

I thought about all the times Tommy and I had been called in because of something he'd done, and realized that he was right.

"So we have to get to where we first came in?" I asked. "But that's where all the vampires were."

"I'm sure most of them are gone from there by now. They're probably all around the school, looking for us. That's why we have to try and stay one step ahead of them."

"How? We need to find Abby and we have no idea where we're going."

More whispering.

I looked around. Still no idea where it was coming from.

"Deviiiin." A long, slow whisper.

It seemed like it was coming from all around me. I couldn't tell from which direction.

We walked a little further down the hallway.

"Devin . . ."

"Lily?"

"Who are you talking to?" Tommy asked.

"Devin," the whisper said. "Find me, Devin . . ."

"I know where she is," I said.

"What?" Tommy said. "How?"

"Follow me!" I raced up ahead, leading the way with the dart gun.

"Yes, Devin," the whisper repeated. "Help me. Find me."

"Devin!" Tommy called. "You can't just go rushing off like this. It's dangerous. You don't know which one of them might be out there."

Images flashed in my mind, telling me which direction to run. Right. Left. Staircase down. It was like my body took over. I didn't even think about which way to go. I only followed.

"Devin, help me . . ."

My heart raced. "I'm coming, Lily."

At the end of the hallway, was a swinging, double door.

I raced straight toward it and shoved it open, coming face to face with a cafeteria filled with vampires.

Tommy skidded to a stop next to me. He leaned over and whispered, "I think you really need to stop listening to the voices in your head."

CHAPTER TWENTY-ONE

SHOWDOWN AT THE NOSFER ACADEMY CAFETERIA

For a brief moment, nobody moved.

Tommy and I stared across the cafeteria at least fifty vampires, maybe more.

Nobody said a word.

But it only lasted a few seconds.

Because the vampires suddenly seemed to remember that they outnumbered us tremendously.

Tommy grabbed an end of one of the cafeteria tables. "Help me!" I grabbed the other end and we pulled it down, like a barricade, so the top was facing them. He aimed the Super Soaker. "Get down!"

The vampires swarmed, and Tommy fired. He

sprayed in bursts, striking vampire after vampire. Unlike the holy water, this didn't seem to melt them, but it sure did hurt them. Each time one got hit, there was a shriek followed by a sizzling sound.

"Are you just going to sit there?" Tommy yelled. "Or do you plan on helping out?"

He was right. I'd been so caught up in watching him fight that I hadn't moved. "Sorry." I looked around the room and then at the dart gun in my hand. "What do I do? I only have one dart pencil!"

Tommy continued firing. "Open that backpack!"

I unzipped the top and peered inside. At the top were packs of water balloons and a couple of bottles of garlic powder. I moved them aside to see necklaces with different religious symbols on them. I guess he wasn't taking chances. Next to those was another dart gun, but this one had six chambers, each one holding a pencil.

I picked it up. "What the heck is this?"

"A little busy over here!"

"The pencil gun with six chambers."

"Herb and I made it. Use it!"

I took aim and fired.

The pencil shot out, nailing a vampire in the forehead. Instantly, the head exploded, chunks flying out in every direction.

"Whoa!" I yelled. "*That was awesome!*"

"Yeah, we turbo-charged it! Keep firing, it's like a little machine gun."

I held the trigger down and the pencils fired out, one after another, nailing vampire after vampire.

Another vampire's head exploded. One I shot straight into his heart. He burst into flames and melted.

"Reload!" Tommy yelled. "There are more pencils in there."

I dug around and fished out some more.

"Quickly!" Tommy said.

I shoved a pencil into each chamber, and started firing again.

When the pencils ran out, I grabbed the water balloons and threw them as fast as I could.

I lost myself in it, feeling powerful.

I was killing actual vampires.

Tommy growled while firing the Super Soaker.

We were like two action heroes from the movies.

Tommy turned to me. "I'm running out of water!"

I glanced at the backpack. "And I'm running out of filled water balloons."

He searched the cafeteria and pointed. "There! A water fountain!"

It was about fifty feet from us.

"And how do you want to get over there?"

"Grab an end."

I frowned. "What?"

"Grab an end of the table. We're moving! And take the backpack!"

"Are you serious?"

"Stop arguing and let's go!"

I grabbed one of the table ends and helped Tommy drag it across the floor, using it to shield ourselves. We fired as we ran, sending vampires sprawling and exploding in our path, until we reached the fountain and dropped the table again.

Tommy fiddled with the fountain while I held them off by throwing whatever remained of the water balloons.

The vampires closed in.

"Hurry up!" I yelled.

"I'm trying, but this is a low-flow fountain!"

"What are you talking about?"

He exhaled in disgust. "The flow! It's not one of those fountains that shoots out water. It's one of the ones that barely sends anything over the spout. You know, the ones you'd never put your lips near in case you accidentally touch it."

I pushed him out of the way. "Hold them off with whatever you have left."

"What are you going to do?" he asked.

"Just do it!"

Tommy fired into the crowd of vampires.

The water level on the Super Soaker continued to drop.

I grabbed the remaining packages of water balloons and ripped them open, holding each balloon to the water, filling them, and then sprinkling in a little garlic powder afterwards. I quickly tied each one and handed them to Tommy.

Tommy wasted no time, throwing each one almost as soon as he received them.

As tiring as this was, it soon started to work.

The vampires started to thin out and flee.

"That's right!" Tommy screamed. "You better run!"

"Shhhh!" I motioned for him to quiet down. "Don't antagonize them! We don't want them coming back!"

Soon there was nothing left in the cafeteria but us and about two dozen vampire corpses.

I looked around the room at all the piles of smoking ash. "I think we won."

Tommy walked around the room, using the end of Super Soaker to nudge the piles. He nodded. "I knew we would."

"Devin . . ." The whispering.

"Oh, no," I muttered.

"What is it?" Tommy asked.

"The whispers. They're back."

Tommy rolled his eyes. "Not again."

I shook my head. "No, it's a different voice."

Tommy's brow furrowed. "Then, who?"

I held my index finger to my lips. "Shhh!"

"Deeeviiiin."

This time it was clearer. Familiar.

The lights in the cafeteria crackled on and off. A gust of wind blew through.

Suddenly, the cafeteria doors flew open, slamming against the walls.

Tommy and I whirled around to see a small dark silhouette framed in the doorway.

I didn't need to see the face to know who it was.

I already knew.

Abby.

CHAPTER TWENTY-TWO

SOME OF MY BEST FRIENDS ARE VAMPIRES

Tommy and I stared across the cafeteria.

Abby remained still. Her hands were down by her sides. Her eyes locked in on us. They were darker than I'd ever seen. From this distance they looked like two pieces of charcoal.

It took me a moment to realize that Tommy and I were huddled together. We glanced at each other and took a step apart.

Tommy leaned in. "You distract her, and I'll shoot her with the pencil gun."

"Will you stop? We can't shoot her. She's my sister!"

"I didn't mean in the heart! I meant something like with Herb. We just wing her and wound her."

"And if we miss and hit her in the heart?"

Tommy thought a moment. "Well, you know your parents better than I do. Do you think they'll be upset?"

I smacked his chest. "Of course they'll be upset. *She's their daughter!* Think of something else!"

"Maybe another garlic necklace?"

"How do we get it on her?"

"Okay, I got it. You go over there." He pointed, but dropped his arm. His face fell. "Where is she?"

I looked over. The doorway was empty. "Where'd she go?"

He threw his arms up. "How should I know? I just asked you the same thing!"

"She's over here."

Tommy and I spun around, to see Abby standing right behind us, and she wasn't alone.

Herb was next to her.

"Hello, boys. Did you miss me?" He had burns around his neck from where the garlic had been.

Unfortunately, even in a group that contained an eight-year old girl, it was me who had the loudest scream.

Abby stared straight ahead at us, not saying a word. Her face was pale and her eyes were sunken in. Her fangs were out.

There was no denying it. She was a full-fledged vampire.

I held my hands in front of me. "Abby, listen to me, this isn't you."

Tommy whispered out the side of his mouth. "It's not?"

"Not now, Tommy!" I yelled.

"You mean your psychotic little sister isn't normally this creepy?"

"I said *not now!*"

Tommy and I backpedaled while Herb and Abby took steps toward us.

Tommy aimed the Super Soaker at them.

"Don't shoot them!" I hissed. "I mean it."

"We have to do something!" Tommy snapped. "If we don't, they'll kill us!"

"We can't shoot her!" I said while Tommy kept them at bay with the Super Soaker.

Herb smiled. "If you fire at us, your dear little sister will be hit, Devin. How are you going to explain that?"

Tommy waved the Super Soaker at him. "First one I shoot is you, Herb."

He motioned toward Abby. "You waste your time on me, then Abby will get you. She's just becoming a vampire. Her hunger is only going to build."

I gulped and reached into Tommy's backpack. I took

out the single-shot dart gun. I aimed it at Herb. "I'll use this if I have to."

Herb's eyes narrowed. "I don't think you will, but you especially won't use it against her."

Abby took another step toward us.

I swerved the gun at her. "Try me."

Abby stopped, still not speaking.

"You'll get tired," Herb said. "We won't."

Tommy shook his head, keeping the Super Soaker trained on Herb. "Before I do, I'll make sure to shoot the both of you."

Herb smiled. "I guess we'll soon find out."

Tommy glanced at me. "This is so cool! We have a standoff. It's like those western movies!"

I looked at him from the corner of my eye. "What?"

"You know," he said, the excitement clear in his voice. "Nobody can make a move without exposing themselves to danger. I love when they do this in the movies!"

"This isn't the movies!" I said. "This is our lives!"

"All right, no need to be grumpy about it!"

Nobody moved. We just stared at each other for I don't know how long. And honestly, I had no idea what to do. I couldn't just leave Herb and Abby there, but I couldn't stay like this forever.

Herb was right. They had the advantage.

We would tire.

They wouldn't.

I stared into their faces. There were barely any traces of their human selves. It was all vampire now. I thought about all the things that Lily had said about vampire life. There was no way, I could do that to either of them.

Then it hit me.

"Wait," I said. "I have an idea."

I reached for Tommy's backpack again, only this time something grabbed my wrist.

I turned to see Bryce.

His arm had grown back.

There were around ten other vampires with him, surrounding us.

Bryce grinned. "You two are coming with me."

For a moment, I froze. My heart shook like an earthquake going off in my chest.

I jabbed the pencil into his hand.

"Aaaaaargh!" Bryce screamed and released his hold on me.

Tommy whirled and sprayed a stream of garlic water into Bryce's face. Little boils started bubbling up.

Out of the corner of my eye, I saw movement. Herb lunged forward. I spun with the dart gun and pulled the trigger.

It was empty.

The pencil had stayed behind in Bryce's hand.

Herb grabbed Tommy.

"Noooooo!" I yelled.

Herb's mouth opened. Before he could make a move, smoke surrounded us.

The tingling in my body.

Everything disappeared.

In seconds, the mist cleared, and I was standing in some kind of office.

Tommy was next to me. He clenched and unclenched his fists. "What the heck was that?"

I rubbed my hands together. "That's what I was telling you about. It's a vampire trick. It was shown to me by—"

"Hello, Devin."

I sensed her before I saw her. I turned. "Lily."

CHAPTER TWENTY-THREE

TRUTH REVEALED

I stared at Lily, and a million thoughts went through my mind. First, I had to know if she had been behind what had happened earlier.

"Devin!" Lily threw her arms around me. "I'm so glad that you're okay." She squeezed me tightly, like she had been reading my mind.

Tommy rolled his eyes, "Oh, please."

Lily let go of me. "What?"

He snorted. "Nobody's buying it."

Lily turned to me. "What's he talking about?"

"Tonight," I said. "Were you behind this? Us being attacked?"

She cried, "No! I would never do anything to hurt you. I hate that you even think that." She looked down. Her lip quivered. "But unfortunately, I know who was."

Tommy and I glanced at each other.

"What do you mean?" I asked.

The tears started streaming down her face.

She wiped at her eyes. "My dad. He approved this."

"*What?*" I said. "I thought he liked us. That he wanted vampires to live among us. What happened to that?"

She looked at me through tear-filled eyes. "Bryce and Delia got to him. They filled his head with lies, and convinced him you were a threat. To him, to this school . . . to me."

"What?" I said. "I would never hurt you."

"I know that, Devin," she said. "But you have to remember. Vampires have been hunted for years. My dad too. It wouldn't take much convincing for anyone to tell him you wanted to destroy us."

Tommy's brow furrowed. "But what about you? He knew we were friends with you."

She nodded. "That's the problem. They all think I've gotten too close to you. That my judgment isn't great, and that you're a danger to us." She grabbed my hand. "He wanted to destroy all the humans who knew about us and then move us again, Devin! I don't want to move again." Her breathing was rapid. "I like it here. I don't know why he's listening to them, but he is. Right now, I don't know who to trust."

"I know the feeling," Tommy muttered.

"You can trust me, Tommy," she said, and looked away. "But I don't think you can trust my dad."

I stared at the tears on her face. "So what do we do?"

She stepped closer to me and grabbed my shirt. "Devin, I hate saying this, but it's now obvious to me that it's one of them who bit Abby." She paused a moment to compose herself, wiping the tears from her eyes. "They wanted to attack you from within your house. They thought we were getting too close. But I don't know if I'll ever get my dad back. He's done this before. Gone on rampages like this. I thought he was done with it, but I guess he's not."

"Wait a second," I said. "You're saying that he's killed like this before?"

She sniffed back her tears and nodded. "Yes, that's why we move so much. I couldn't tell you before, because he promised that this time was different."

I studied her face, but couldn't tell if she was telling me the truth.

She never changed expression. "I'd never hurt you, Devin. I thought for sure he'd let this be."

Tommy blew air up from his bottom lip and turned to her. "So, what do you want us to do?"

She looked down. "I don't know. I just want to fly away from here. Everything is such a mess, and it's all my fault."

Tommy turned to me. "I don't buy it." He reached

into the backpack and pulled out the garlic powder. "I say we eliminate her."

Lily's eyes widened. "I wasn't responsible. I promise."

I grabbed the garlic powder from him. "Will you stop it?"

He threw his hands up. "You're making a huge mistake!"

I ignored him. "Lily, if something does happen to the main vampire won't all the other people in his line change back?"

She nodded slowly. "Yes."

"And wouldn't that make you a human girl again?"

She looked up. Her tears stopped. Her eyes sparkled a moment. "Yes, but . . ." It came out as a whisper. She ran her hand down my arm until she grasped my hand. "I don't know what to say to you. He's my dad." She walked over to a chair behind the desk, wiped her eyes on her sleeve, and looked back to me. "Maybe if only Bryce and Delia were gotten rid of, Abby would turn back. My dad's not the one who bit her. He would've sent one of them."

"But what about you?" I asked. "You'd still be a vampire."

She nodded. "I know. But I've been doing it for so long that it's my life now. Maybe I can talk to my dad. Make him stop this and see reason."

Tommy paced around the desk, eyeing Lily the whole time, like a detective interrogating a suspect. "So, where is your dad now?"

Lily's face twisted. "I don't know. I'm hiding from him. He would hate it if he knew I was telling you all of this."

Tommy walked behind her, where she couldn't see him, and motioned to me. He pantomimed hammering a stake into someone.

I glared at him.

Lily sprang up from her seat. "Listen, my dad's a lot more powerful than me. If he even knew I was talking to you, I might be next, and I'm his daughter. Maybe it's best that you just take Abby and run."

"I can't run!" I said. "She's a vampire. I can't take her back home like this!"

"Then we're going to have to find one of them. I'll help you. But if my dad finds out, I'll be in just as much danger as you. Maybe more. If there's one thing vampires hate more than anything, it's going against the clan." Her face was sad, desperate. Even though she was there to help us, she was the one who looked like she needed rescuing.

I gave her a small smile. "Thank you, Lily. Where do you want to start?"

Suddenly, her face froze, contorting with fear and pain. Before she could answer, black smoke surrounded us.

It wasn't like with Lily before. This was darker. Thicker. A burnt smell surrounded us. She reached out to me. I tried to grab her hand, but there was nothing there.

The smoke enveloped everything.

"Lily?" I shouted. I couldn't see in any direction. I waved my hand in front of my face, trying to clear the air.

Finally, after a few moments, the smoke started to disappear.

Lily was gone.

In her place was Mr. Moroi.

He was standing between us and the door.

Out in the hall we heard the snarls of other vampires. *How had they found us so fast?*

"There you are!" he said. "I've been looking everywhere for you." He pointed to the door. "I'm clouding their senses. Nobody's going to take the two of you from me."

Tommy flipped open the garlic powder bottle and held it in front of him. His hands trembled. "I'm warning you, stay back!"

Mr. Moroi's brow creased. "Stay back?"

I nodded. "Yeah, we heard all about how you teamed up with Bryce and Delia."

His face fell. "Delia? Who talked to you about Delia?"

Alarm bells went off. I had said too much. I didn't want him knowing it was Lily that ratted him out.

"We figured it out," I said. "Now, leave us alone, and turn Abby and Herb back, or we'll be forced to kill you."

Mr. Moroi held his hands in front of him. "Boys, I'm sorry to tell you this, but you've been played for fools. It's probably my fault, but there's something you need to know about Delia. She's—"

Suddenly, his head snapped back. There was a howl of pain and then a gurgling sound. He started convulsing. A black stain started to spread on his shirt.

I quickly realized that it was coming from the wooden stake that had pierced his chest.

Mr. Moroi shook violently, and then started to melt. First his face, down to his skull. Then his eyes and body. In seconds, all that was left was a greenish and black puddle on the floor.

Tommy and I stood there with our mouths open.

I looked up and my heart dropped. Suddenly, everything made sense. The sounds I heard in the bushes. The wiping away of the garlic powder on the floor. The eyes up in the tree.

Herb's words rang in my head. "When you get a supernatural being angry, they won't stop at anything until they get even."

In his hand he held a large wooden stake.

Actually, it wasn't in his hand.

It was in his paw.

"Mr. Flopsy-Ears."

CHAPTER TWENTY-FOUR

WE MEET AGAIN

I wanted to scream, but I was too stunned to make a sound. Everything inside me went cold. "I thought you were dead!"

Mr. Flopsy-Ears reached down and moved some of the fur from his belly to the side.

There was a long row of stitches sewn across.

He turned the stake and pointed it at me.

"Tommy!" I yelled. "Do something!"

"I don't know what to do!" Tommy screamed. "I have a ton of vampire stuff, not bunny stuff."

Mr. Flopsy-Ears leaped at me, holding the stake out in front.

I jumped out of the way just before he struck the wall behind me. The stake briefly lodged in the wall before he yanked it out.

I grabbed a chair and held it in front of me like a shield.

Mr. Flopsy-Ears whirled around to face me.

"Stay back!" I pushed the chair in the air at him, like I was a lion-tamer.

Mr. Flopsy-Ears scurried behind the desk.

"Will you do something!?" I shouted at Tommy.

He grabbed a chair. "What's Mr. Flopsy-Ears doing here?"

"How should I know? I didn't stop to ask him."

He looked around the office. "Where is he?"

I darted my eyes back and forth, searching. "I have no idea!"

I heard the sounds of little paws scurrying across the room.

Tommy grabbed my shoulder. "I don't see him."

I kept turning, trying to follow the sounds, but it seemed like it was coming from all directions. "I don't know. He could be anywhere."

"You don't have anything in the backpack that we can use?"

Tommy rummaged through it. "I don't know! We have no potion. No holy water. No anything!"

"What about the garlic water?" I asked.

"*Why would garlic water work on a stuffed animal?*"

"How should I know? I'm just asking. You're the one who knows all this stuff."

Tommy lifted the pencil gun and aimed it around the room.

I motioned toward it. "Will that work?"

He shook his head. "No. But maybe it'll slow him down a little."

More scurrying.

"Let's get out of here," I said.

Suddenly, something banged into the door.

We jumped and spun around.

On the other side of the frosted glass there were shadows, clawing at it.

The door rattled.

Tommy reached into the backpack. "I only have a few water balloons left."

"And garlic powder?"

He checked the backpack. "Around half a bottle."

I closed my eyes for a moment. "That's not going to last very long."

"What do you want me to do? Don't blame me!"

"I'm not blaming you. I'm just saying that you should've brought more."

He turned to me. "Well, that sounds like you're blaming me. If it wasn't for me we wouldn't have any of this stuff to begin with."

"I know! I'm just saying—"

Someone whistled.

Tommy and I whirled.

Mr. Flopsy-Ears was standing on the desk, holding the stake above his head like a spear.

He wiggled his eyebrows a couple of times.

"Oh, no," I said. "I think he's going to—"

He reared his paw back and let the stake fly. It sailed through the air toward us, right at our heads.

I grabbed Tommy. "Duck!"

We dropped just in time, as the spear flew over our heads.

Too late, I realized he wasn't throwing it at us.

It crashed through the door's window, sending shards of frosted glass raining down on top of us.

We looked up to see a dozen vampires staring back at us.

CHAPTER TWENTY-FIVE

A DJ SAVED MY LIFE TONIGHT

We jumped back from the door as the vampires clawed at the air.

Tommy thrust his arm into the backpack and pulled out the cross.

The vampires hissed, but kept their distance.

Tommy and I stood back to back. He held the cross out to the vampires while I held up the pencil gun to Mr. Flopsy-Ears.

Mr. Flopsy-Ears took a step toward us, smiling.

"What are we going to do?" I asked.

"Okay," Tommy said. "The way I see it is that we have some things to hold off vampires, but we don't really have anything to fight off demonic stuffed animals."

"So what does that mean?"

"It means on the count of three, we get ready to run."

I peeked back over my shoulder. "What are you talking about?" I looked around the office. "There's no place to go!"

"One."

"Don't! I mean it!"

"Two."

"Stop counting! You never tell me what the plan is before we do it!"

"There's no time! Three!"

Tommy whipped garlic powder at the vampires and yanked open the door. "Let's go!"

"*Into the vampires?*"

An object whooshed by my ear and hit the wall with a *thunk*. I didn't even look to see what it was.

With a loud bunny shriek, Mr. Flopsy-Ears leaped from the desk and landed on my back. He grabbed my hair like the reins of a horse.

"Ow!" I screamed and smacked him off.

I wasn't going to give him another shot. I wasted no time. While the vampires were clearing the garlic from their eyes, I burst through them, knocking several to the ground.

Tommy was already twenty feet in front of me down the hall.

"Wait!" I yelled.

"No!" he shouted back. "You catch up!"

I sprinted as fast as I could, trying to make up ground. I had no idea where he was going, and unfortunately, I didn't think he did either.

Finally, I caught up to him as we turned the corner to the next hall. We skidded to a stop. We were back in the lobby, where the whole night started.

Thankfully, no vampires were there, but lots of tables and chairs were overturned. Dishes littered the floor along with the bodies of some of the guests.

Blood was everywhere.

I covered my mouth. "Ugh." I started to heave.

"C'mon!" Tommy yelled. "We don't have time for you to be sick." He pointed to the bodies. "Or that'll be us!" He ran to the front of the school and motioned for me to follow.

The door was locked, but through the glass I could see the metal shutters that the DJ had triggered with the remote control.

I yanked on the door, but it wouldn't budge. "It's locked."

Tommy looked around. "Wait, I got it." He ran over, grabbed a chair, and flung it into the door. The glass shattered, shards flying out in every direction. He used the chair to knock out the remaining pieces stuck to the doorframe before pushing against the metal shutter.

It had some give to it, but wouldn't open.

"Aaargh!" he screamed. "We're stuck!"

I fished the iPhone out of my pocket. "Still no reception." I glanced at the clock. "It's already five in the morning! We've been here the whole night! My mom is going to kill me!"

"She's not going to kill you! After she hears what you went through, she's never going to yell at you about anything ever again."

"You don't know my mom."

Tommy rattled the shutters. "Never mind that. Look for something that we can use to get out while I see if I can get this open."

"Like what?"

"How should I know? That's why you're looking."

I sighed. He always did this to me. Always, half-telling. Never giving the full information.

I started searching all the tables.

What the heck could we use to open a metal shutter?

From the distance, I heard shrieks getting closer.

It sounded like . . .

"Bats," I muttered. "Tommy, they're coming!"

He rattled the shutters again. "I can't get it open!"

"We don't have time for you to get it open! We have to get out of here!"

The shrieking grew louder.

"Pssst," someone whispered.

I scanned the area.

"Devin!" Another whisper.

"Lily?"

"No! Down here."

I followed the voice and saw Herb waving to me from under the DJ table.

He had the long blue tablecloth bunched around his neck. "Quick, get under here!"

I took a step back. "No way! You're a vampire!"

He shook his head. "No, not anymore! You must've killed the one who turned me. I reverted back."

I thought back to all the vampires we had killed that night. "Maybe, but it could be that Mr. Moroi is dead."

His eyes widened. "You killed Mr. Moroi!"

"Well, no. Mr. Flopsy-Ears did."

"*Mr. Flopsy-Ears?*"

I nodded. "Yeah, he's back."

His mouth was a thin line across his face. "That's not good."

"Tell me about it! He almost killed me!"

He frowned. "It's just as I thought. Just what I told you about supernatural creatures. Mr. Flopsy-Ears is now a sworn enemy of yours and needs to be the one responsible for your death. He simply won't tolerate you dying unless he has a hand in it."

"A sworn enemy?" I said. "I'm too young to have a sworn enemy."

Herb waved his hand in front of his face. "We can discuss that later! Right now, you need to get under here! They'll be here at any moment."

"Are you sure you're not a vampire?"

He held the tablecloth up. "Get under here!"

"Okay, okay!" I called out. "Tommy!"

He looked over.

I motioned for him. "Get under here, fast!"

"What? Why?"

"No explanations now. Just get over here!"

He ran across the room and slid under the table.

I jumped under and pulled the tablecloth down, moments before we heard the savage sounds of snarling fill the lobby.

Herb held his index finger to his lips.

He didn't have to tell me twice. I kept quiet. Too afraid to make a sound.

All around us, there were growls.

I mouthed, "What do we do?"

Herb held his hand up. Soon there were the sounds of yelping, like wounded dogs.

"Devin?"

"Abby?" I whispered.

Tommy, Herb, and I glanced at each other.

"Devin, where are you?"

I reached for the tablecloth but Herb snatched my wrist. "Don't!"

"I saw you run in this direction, and I hid until the vampires left," Abby said. "I'm not a vampire anymore. I turned back."

I looked at Herb. "She changed back, like you did. Maybe we killed the one who bit her also?"

Herb's brow furrowed. "I guess it's possible. But when I turned back I didn't see her near me."

"That doesn't mean anything!" I said. "We have to go out to her."

Herb shook his head. "Wait."

"Devin, please!" Abby's voice cracked. "I'm scared."

"It's a trap!" Tommy said. "Your sister never gets scared of anything." He held up the pencil gun. "I think we have to eliminate her."

I knocked his arm down. "Will you stop with the eliminating already!" I grabbed the bottom of the table cloth. "Just one quick look."

I lifted the bottom of the tablecloth and peeked out.

From my angle I could see just her legs. She wasn't moving.

There was nobody else around.

I turned back to Herb and Tommy. "She's alone. We have to get her now!"

Tommy frowned. "I don't like it."

"So what do you want me to do?" I asked. "Just leave her there?"

Tommy raised an eyebrow. "Wait, is that an option? Because I can't tell if you're being serious right now."

"No, I'm not being serious. We have to go save her because we're not staying under the table waiting for them to find us."

Tommy bit his lip. "Are those the only two choices we have?"

"Listen to me. Those shutters are down, so there's nowhere else to go." I pointed at the tablecloth. "Unless we get out of here we'll be trapped, and this hiding spot isn't going to fool anybody for very long."

Herb sighed. "Okay, I know we have to save her, but the problem is we're just taking her word about what happened."

"She sounds normal," I said. "Well, normal for Abby."

"Let's be safe," Herb said. "Devin, you take the cross." He handed it me. "Tommy, you take the gun, and I'll take the Super Soaker."

"Wait! Why do you get the Super Soaker?" Tommy asked.

"Because I'm the one who brought it." He snatched it from Tommy.

Tommy pouted. "Aww, man! Fine!" He took out a pencil gun from the backpack.

"Are we ready?" Herb asked.

I took a deep breath and nodded.

He turned to Tommy. "And you?"

Tommy lifted the pencil gun. "Ready."

Herb grabbed the bottom of the tablecloth. "Let's go save Abby and kill some vampires."

CHAPTER TWENTY-SIX

LET THE SUNSHINE IN

If I was going to be honest, somewhere in the back of my mind, I always had the feeling that Abby would be responsible for killing me.

And that was even before she had turned into a vampire.

Now, I had no idea if she was still one or not. But when we jumped out from under the DJ's table and were surrounded by over a hundred vampires, it kind of brought all those other memories flooding back.

Abby stood motionless, staring straight ahead.

If that had been her calling out to me it would've been a fantastic trick, since she didn't seem to be aware of anything going on around her.

All around us were snarling, hissing vampires, with about a five-foot invisible barrier on all sides. Herb,

Tommy, and I held them at bay, but there were so many of them. Every time one lunged at us, I thrust the cross out and it turned away.

I wasn't sure if they didn't realize how easily they could have overwhelmed us, or if none of them wanted to be the first one sacrificed. Either way, we couldn't stay like this forever. Eventually they would figure this out. We would get tired. I wasn't sure if they could.

"What do we do?" I asked.

"Keep in formation!" Herb yelled.

Tommy scooted back some. "I told you we should've left her!"

"Shut up, Tommy!" I said.

I glanced over at Abby. She was still expressionless. It was like she was in a daze. Hypnotized.

Somebody whistled. The vampires all stopped snarling and backed away.

There was silence.

"What's going on?" I whispered.

Suddenly, I heard footsteps echoing throughout the lobby. A path cleared.

Bryce came into view. He walked over to Abby and put his hand on her shoulder. "Hello, Devin." He smiled.

"Where's Lily?" I asked.

"Don't worry about Lily." He smiled. His fangs were out. "She'll be just fine. As a matter of fact, I sent Delia after her." He laughed. "But let's talk about this little one." He rested his hand on Abby's head. "Watch this. Hello, Devin." He said it, but it was in Abby's voice. "Help me, Devin, I'm surrounded."

The vampires laughed.

Bryce shrugged. "You like that one? It's quite simple, really. We can impersonate voices. Vampires are natural actors. Makes the theater school a logical fit. A great way to lure humans over. Never a good idea to be their friends. Mr. Moroi forgot that, and look what it got him." He pointed to us. "Moroi wanted to trust them and look what happened. They killed him!"

"Wait!" I lifted my arms. "We didn't kill him! I swear!"

Bryce laughed again. "Nice try. We saw your handiwork in that room. I told him you couldn't be trusted, he didn't listen."

"Wait," I said. "He didn't want to eat us?"

"*Eat you?*" Bryce shrieked. "He practically wanted you to be the lead in his next play." He frowned. "Sickening. But still, he didn't deserve to die at the hands of some human garbage."

"We didn't kill him!" I said. "It was Mr. Flopsy-Ears!"

Yeah, I heard how stupid that sounded too.

The vampires grew silent.

Bryce's brow furrowed. "Who?"

I was too far in to stop now. "A murderous stuffed bunny."

Yeah, we were dead.

The room erupted in laughter until Bryce quieted everyone down. "I never agreed with him about things, but he deserved better than to be killed by the likes of you. Thankfully, we'll have some new management in this place. But first things first."

Before my eyes, his fingernails grew into sharp-looking points. He traced one slowly over Abby's head and down her face until he reached her throat.

I clenched the cross in my hand. "Stay away from her."

Bryce smirked. "Or what?"

All of the vampires laughed again.

Bryce snapped his fingers and they grew instantly silent. He turned back to me. "Devin, by the time you'd reach me I could have her throat slit many times over." He held up his hand. "But I won't kill her if I don't have to." He patted her head. "As a matter of fact, she's a natural." He took a step toward me. "I haven't seen a girl take to being a vampire this naturally since . . ." He shrugged. "Well, since Lily."

Her name froze me over. I scanned the room. "Where is she?"

He snarled. "I told you, don't worry about her! We'll take care of her later. For now, we have to deal with you." He shook his head. "You know we can't let you leave. Not with what you've seen."

"We won't tell anyone about you or this school," I said. "I promise. Just please let us go."

He clicked his tongue. "Devin, we can't trust you now. You know too much." He grinned. "So you have a couple of choices." He held up two fingers. "Either you come join us and be a part of our clan . . . or we kill you."

"What was the first one again?" Tommy asked.

"Quiet!" I hissed, and turned back to Bryce. "We don't want to be vampires. We want to go home to our family. Please."

Bryce shook his head. "That's not one of the options, Devin." He put his hand around Abby's neck and tightened his grip.

Black blood trickled from her throat.

"Stop it!" I yelled.

"Join us or die!" he screamed.

"Please!" Tears started to well in my eyes.

He reared his other hand back. "You'd better think fast."

I frantically scanned the area, searching for either a way out or something that we could use against them, when I saw the remote on the DJ's desk.

I glanced at the shutters.

A small sliver of light at the spot where Tommy had bent.

"It's daytime," I whispered.

"What?" Tommy said.

"I'll give you 'til three," Bryce said. "And then your sister says bye-bye."

I turned to the DJ's table and saw two turntables, a microphone, and the remote. I turned to Herb. "I have an idea."

"Well, you better make it fast," Herb said.

"One."

The vampires started hissing and closing in.

"That remote that the DJ used to close the shutters. It's on the table."

"WHAT?" Herb and Tommy said simultaneously.

"So use it now!" Tommy said.

"Two."

"I can't! If Abby is a vampire, it'll kill her."

"But—" Tommy started to say.

"No time!" I yelled. "You'll know when."

"And . . ." Bryce said.

"Just do it!" I grabbed the edge of the table cloth and yanked it out from under the turntables, sending them crashing to the ground. The mic and remote flew up into the air. I didn't stop to see what would happen.

I rushed straight at Bryce.

His eyes widened. The vampires hissed, turned their attention to me, and attacked. There were bursts of sharp, jolting pain from where they clawed at me, but I pushed through.

I leaped straight at Bryce and Abby.

He released his hold on her and took a step back. He snarled and held his claws out.

I knocked Abby to the ground and wrapped the tablecloth around her.

"Now!" I screamed.

Nothing happened.

The vampires swarmed me. Searing, sharp pain went through me as several vampires clawed into me. My arms, shoulders, chest, and legs.

"Now!" I yelled again.

What the heck is taking them so long?

"Stop!" Bryce yelled. "He's mine!" He pulled several of them off and grabbed me by my throat. He bared his fangs. "I'm not going to let them eat you. You've killed way too many of my friends tonight. Instead, I'll make you a mindless, zombie slave. You'll be serving us for an eternity. Helpless to stop it. You'll watch as we devour your family, your friends, your—"

"*What is going on?*" I screamed.

Bryce dug his nails into my throat.

I grabbed his wrist, but he was too strong.

With his other hand, he held his index finger to his lips. "Shhh! It'll all be over soon." He opened his mouth wide. His fangs grew before me. "Goodbye, Devin."

Suddenly, a buzzer went off.

Bryce and the other vampires all whirled toward the front. Fear was carved into their faces.

Instantly, the shutters popped open, bathing the room in sunlight. It reflected off the chandelier and shot its way throughout the room. Vampire shrieks filled the air. The sound of sizzling, like bacon frying in a pan.

Smoke everywhere.

All around me, vampires either melted or exploded, sending vampire chunks shooting out in all directions. Bryce's face melted like hot candle wax. First the skin, then the flesh, until finally the eyes.

A skeleton in clothes collapsed to the ground and splintered off across the floor.

I looked around the room. There were vampire puddles and parts all over.

Tommy and Herb raced to my side. Tommy put his hand on my shoulder. "Are you okay?"

I looked up at him. *"What took the two of you so long?"*

"It's not my fault!" Tommy said. "When you knocked the remote off the table, it hit the floor and the batteries rolled out. Herb and I had to crawl around looking for them."

"I must say," Herb said. "It's not so easy finding a battery among blood and body parts. It's like the proverbial needle in a haystack."

The tablecloth started to squirm.

We all turned toward it.

"Do you think we can take the tablecloth off?" I asked.

Abby snarled.

Herb glanced at me. "That sounds like a 'no.'"

I ran my hand through my hair. "I don't understand. Why is she still a vampire? How is it possible? One of them had to be the one who bit her. We killed all of them, didn't we?"

Tommy glanced at Herb and then turned back to me. "That one, Delia. She wasn't here."

I shook my head. "No, she's got to be one of these. We have to check."

Tommy looked around the room. "Check what? They're all puddles of vampire goo, there's nothing left for us to check."

I took another look. "So what do we do?"

Herb leaned in. "Considering that we don't know if there are any more vampires here, and we also have Mr. Flopsy-Ears running around somewhere, I suggest we get out of here fast!"

"But what about Abby?" I asked.

Herb pointed to the rolled-up tablecloth. "If she's still a vampire that means the one who bit her is still alive. It also means that they'll be back. Vampires don't turn someone without making them part of their clan."

I closed my eyes for a moment. "So that means another vampire will attack us?"

Herb shrugged. "I don't know, but either way we have to be ready for them, just in case." He motioned to Abby. "In the meantime, let's get her to the car."

CHAPTER TWENTY-SEVEN

My Sister the Vampire

We carried Abby in the rolled-up tablecloth out to Herb's car.

Never in my life did it feel as good to have the sun hit my face as it did in that moment. Everyone always talks about the sun bringing life, and I have to say, it sure saved ours.

Abby squirmed inside.

"Can she even breathe in this thing?" I asked.

"I hope so," Herb said. "But we have no choice right now. Just get her in the car."

We loaded her into the back seat, and I sat next to her.

Herb and Tommy jumped into the front and we all closed the doors behind us.

Herb roared the engine to life and peeled out. "Okay, the windows are tinted. It should be safe to take the tablecloth off of her."

"Are you sure?" I asked.

Herb shrugged. "Reasonably sure. Like eighty-five percent."

"Herb, those aren't good enough odds for my sister's life!"

Herb glanced at me in the rearview mirror. "Okay, okay. I'm pretty sure it's a lot closer to ninety."

I had to admit, Herb had a point. It was pretty dark.

"Please, let this work," I whispered as I grabbed the bottom of the tablecloth.

Slowly I lifted it, inch by inch, until the whole thing was off of her.

Abby never moved.

She sat there, staring straight ahead.

I snapped my fingers in front of her eyes.

Nothing.

"Herb, what's going on with her?"

"She was turned. It always affects everyone differently. Sometimes you turn right away, sometimes your body is trying to reject it, so you go in and out of a catatonic state. One minute she's active, and the next it looks like she's in a coma."

"Well, how do we fix her?"

Herb was silent for a moment. "The only way I

know for sure is to kill the vampire who bit her, and I would've thought we did that tonight, but apparently not. I don't know of any other methods right now, but if it's out there we'll find it." He peeked back in the mirror. "The only thing we have to worry about is for when the vampire who turned her comes back to get her."

My heart pounded. "And when will that be?"

Herb shrugged. "Vampires like to keep their clans with them. Whoever did it will be back. But don't worry, we'll be ready for whoever it is."

I fell back in my seat. "Great. I have a vampire after me."

"Oh," Tommy said. "And don't forget about Mr. Flopsy-Ears."

"I didn't forget, thanks. I don't even know how he's still alive, let alone after me."

Tommy snorted. "You even told me yourself you never killed him. He was still alive when you left him last time. Why should he be dead now? He's a stuffed animal. You really have to make sure they're destroyed. Otherwise they can just sew themselves right up."

Herb nodded. "Yes, as I already mentioned, Mr. Flopsy-Ears is a supernatural creature. When you cross a supernatural creature, they stop at nothing to get even. That's why Mr. Flopsy-Ears wiped the garlic away. So the vampires could get in."

"But he could've just killed me himself."

"Think about it," Tommy said. "What's a more gruesome way to die? Killed in your sleep, or devoured by vampires?" He shrugged. "You gotta admit, Mr. Flopsy-Ears has flair."

I glared at Herb in the rearview mirror. "Well, then why isn't he after you? You're the one who created him!"

Herb chuckled. "Oh, I'm sure I'm on his list, but you're the one who defeated him last time. There's a pecking order, which you're at the top of. Should you get killed, then I'd start to worry, but until then . . . I'm probably okay."

I sighed. "Thanks, Herb, that makes me feel a whole lot better. Now, I have vampires *and* a psycho stuffed bunny after me. And that's if my parents don't kill me first."

"Devin, please relax," Herb said. "I'll speak to your parents. As the adult chaperone, I feel it is my duty to take responsibility for this. I'll speak to them and allay their fears."

I rolled my eyes. "Herb, even with all your warlock tricks you don't have enough magic to get me out of this one so easily."

Herb kept driving. "Devin, after they hear what happened they'll be so relieved that you're safe they'll both be forgiving of any minor transgressions."

I motioned toward Abby. "And how do I explain her?"

Tommy glanced at her. "Don't say anything, unless they bring it up first."

"She's staring at nothing, and not talking!"

Tommy shrugged. "I don't know. I think it's kind of an improvement."

"Leave me alone. You're not helping." My phone buzzed in my pocket. "My phone has reception again! Maybe it's them now." I fished it out. My brow furrowed. "That's weird."

"What are you talking about?" Tommy asked.

I flashed the screen toward him. "We were gone all night, and there's not one message or text from my parents."

Tommy smiled. "That's awesome! And you were worried we'd be in trouble. They probably didn't even notice that we were gone."

"We never came home. How could they not notice?"

Tommy's expression turned sad. "Oh, wow, Devin. I'm sorry. This is a rotten way to find out that your parents don't love you."

"Will you cut it out? My parents love me! Something's wrong."

"Well, we're almost to your house," Herb said. "We'll find out everything then."

Tommy and Herb went on yammering for the rest of the ride, but I stayed silent. I had no idea what I'd find when I got home, and my thoughts kept drifting back to Lily. Did Bryce do something to her?

I didn't even want to think about it, but I couldn't stop.

Something had happened to Lily.

CHAPTER TWENTY-EIGHT

HOME UNSWEET HOME

Herb backed into my driveway, next to our minivan. It shielded us a little, made it easier to wrap Abby in the tablecloth again and carry her into the house. I had seen movies like this, where mobsters did the same things to dead bodies, and exactly like in the movies, nobody stopped to ask us any questions.

I unlocked the door and pushed. It creaked open.

Inside, there was silence. Not only that, it was dark. Unbelievably dark.

"Hello?" I called out.

Nothing. Chills ran down my back. Every instinct screamed at me to run, but I needed to check it out for myself. I glanced back out the door. It was sunny, and even though I had just seen our car, I double-checked to make sure it was there.

We all stood there in the doorway, nobody making a move to go in.

"We can't just stand here in the sun," Herb said. "Even though Abby is wrapped, we can't take chances of it getting through."

"Okay, okay," I said. "It's just that something's wrong in there."

Herb stepped inside. "We'll investigate, but we must get her inside."

We carried Abby in and set her down on the couch.

Herb pointed. "Shut the door before we unwrap the tablecloth."

I ran over and closed it. The room turned pitch dark.

"Why is it so dark in here?" I said.

I turned on my cell phone flashlight and reached for the light switch on the wall.

Click.

Click.

I flipped it back and forth, again and again.

Click. Click. Click.

"What's going on?" I said.

"Your parents must've not paid the bill," Tommy said.

"They pay the bills!" I snapped and realized that I really had no idea. "I think."

"This has nothing to do with the bills," Herb said. "Somebody did this." He yanked the curtains back to reveal the windows were painted black.

Abby started to squirm. Snarling came from within.

"Uh oh," I muttered.

"Quick, give me the garlic powder!" Herb said.

Tommy reached into his backpack and tossed the bottle to Herb. "There's not a lot left."

He opened it and sprinkled the remaining powder around the couch. "That should hold her for now." He looked around the room. "But since she snapped to like that it leads me to believe that our vampire is already here."

I grabbed my wrist to stop my arm from trembling. Now if I could only steady my legs. "What do we do?"

"Well, first things first." He waved his hands in a circle, and a little ball of light appeared. "That'll help us see a little better."

"Can't you do the whole thing?" I asked.

He shook his head. "There's definitely vampire magic at work here. This is the best that I can do." Herb listened for sounds. "I think we have to split up and check every room."

"What?" Tommy said. "No way! That's an awful idea. You never split up! Don't you watch horror movies?" He smacked his hand. "When you split up, bad things happen. It's Horror 101. The stupid teens split up and then they're picked off one by one." He shook his head. "There's no way. We're sticking together."

I nodded and pointed to Tommy. "Yeah, I'm with him."

Herb looked around again. "Okay, I see your point. Let's go together from room to room."

"*Devin* . . ."

My blood froze.

We turned around and all three of us yelped and jumped into each other's arms.

Standing on the couch was Abby in full-blown vampire mode. Actually, she wasn't standing. She was hovering around a foot above it.

"I'm hungry, Devin." Her fangs were out.

"Okay, everyone calm down," Herb said. "She can't leave that garlic circle."

I pointed to the couch. "What are you talking about? She can fly right over it!"

"No, sirree!" Herb said. "She can't cross that circle. It's like an invisible barrier all the way up." He walked toward the couch. "Watch this." He circled the couch.

Abby lunged at him, but peeled back each time once she reached a certain point.

Herb turned to us and smiled. "See? Barrier." He motioned for us to follow. "Now, everyone grab a weapon, and c'mon."

I grabbed the cross; Tommy, the pencil gun; and Herb, the Super Soaker.

Abby continued hissing, but we ignored it and started walking.

"When I get out of here, Devin . . ." She pointed to me, and then snapped her fangs.

I gulped and pushed Herb and Tommy along.

Using the lights from our cell phones, and the ball of light in Herb's hand, we searched everywhere on the first floor. The kitchen, the family room, the guest room, and nothing.

We stopped at the foot of the stairs and looked up. The second floor seemed like it was miles away.

"Okay," Herb said. "You go up, and we'll follow right behind you."

"What?" I hissed. "You're the adult."

"It's your house," he whispered.

Tommy nodded. "He's right about that."

"Will you shut up?" I said. "We all go together."

Tommy frowned. "Fine!"

The three of us squeezed into the narrow staircase and took each step, one at a time, holding our weapons out in front of us.

"This reminds me of the scene in *Psycho*," Tommy said. "Where the mom was waiting at the top of the steps with a knife."

We stopped walking.

"What'd you have to say that for?" I said.

He shrugged. "What? I need to talk when I'm nervous. It helps keep my mind off how dangerous the situation is."

"Please, shut up!" I said.

"I must agree with Devin," Herb said. "Besides, the staircase in *The Exorcist* was much scarier."

"What's with the two of you?" I said. "No more discussing scary movies!"

"Fine!" Tommy said. "What a grouch."

We climbed the stairs, step by step, until we reached the second-floor landing. It was dark up here, too. All the windows were painted black. It was an eerie feeling, being in my own house and worried about what else might be there.

Abby's door and my door were only partially open, but Mom and Dad's was open wide.

My heart galloped in my chest.

I needed to quiet it down.

Breathe, Devin. Breathe.

We all glanced at each other before creeping silently toward Mom and Dad's room.

Our arms were extended in front of us.

One hand holding the lights, the other the weapons.

As soon as we reached Mom and Dad's doorway, I saw them.

They were lying on their bed, not moving.

I rushed in, forgetting for a moment about vampires, Abby, and everything else I had been worried about.

Mom and Dad both had their eyes open and were staring straight up at the ceiling.

"They're in the same state that Abby was," I said.

"Look!" Tommy pointed and held the cell phone light to their necks.

Both of them had several bite marks.

"My whole family is going to be vampires," I whispered.

Herb put his hand on my back. "Look, there are even little trickles of blood. This is recent. I bet whoever did it is still here."

Everyone quickly flashed their lights around the room, crossing the paths of the beams.

"Okay, stop!" Herb said. "Calm down! Let's be organized about this. Tommy, you look under the bed."

He shook his head. "There is *no* way I'm looking under that bed."

"We can't all do everything together," Herb said.

"Then you look under the bed," Tommy said.

Herb grunted. "Very well. Let's look under the bed together."

We all eyed each other before slowly lowering ourselves to the ground.

Herb counted to three on his fingers.

Tommy pointed the pencil gun, and Herb pointed the Super Soaker.

Herb yanked the blanket up.

Tommy fired.

The pencil shot all the way under the bed to the other side of the room.

Nothing was there.

"Oops," Tommy said. "Sorry."

"Go get the pencil!" Herb whispered. "We can't waste ammunition!"

"Okay, okay!" He crawled over to the spot where the pencil had landed and reloaded.

We finished the bathroom and closets, and no one was there.

Herb exhaled. "Okay, that means it's one of two spots. Abby's room or yours."

"Devin . . ." More whispers.

I whirled around the room. "Did you hear that?"

Tommy cocked his head. "Hear what?"

I turned to Herb. He shook his head.

More whispers. I whirled again.

Nothing.

"Follow me," I said, and walked out of the room into the hall.

A cool breeze hit my face.

I held the light up. Dark everywhere. Where was it coming from?

"Your room first?" Herb asked.

I paused a moment and then nodded.

We stopped outside my door.

"Devin..."

"The vampire's in my room," I whispered.

Herb and Tommy crowded around me.

I swallowed hard and gently pushed the door open.

We peered in. All I saw were shadows. I couldn't even make out everything in the room.

Herb leaned close. "Let's be careful. Huddle close and stay back to back. Anyone sees anything, say it fast."

Tommy and I nodded.

I took the first step in.

A cold, tingling sensation shot through me as I crossed the threshold. Suddenly, a fierce blast of cold wind blew from my room and knocked Herb and Tommy back into the hall. I spun around, but the door slammed shut. I ran over and tried to yank it open, but it wouldn't budge. I rattled it a few times, but nothing.

"C'mon," I muttered.

"Hello, Devin,"

My breath caught. I closed my eyes.

I glanced back over my shoulder, before I turned fully around.

A red glow surrounded her. She hovered a few feet above the floor.

I didn't know whether to be happy or scared out of my mind.

"Lily..."

CHAPTER TWENTY-NINE

RELATIONSHIPS WITH VAMPIRES AREN'T EASY

For months, the sight of Lily had sent my heart racing. I always used to wish she'd look my way, or just come by and say hi. Little did I know that I would have been much better off if none of that had ever happened. Because, back then, I had no idea that she was a blood-thirsty vampire, intent on turning my family into obedient, bloodsucking slaves.

"I thought you died."

She shrugged. "It'll take a lot more than that to kill me."

"But you were so upset when I saw you. You were crying."

She bowed. "Acting." She smiled. "And I've been able to practice and rehearse my craft for a very long time."

There was pounding on the door.

"Devin!" Tommy yelled. "Are you okay in there? What's going on?"

"Lily's in here!" I yelled back over my shoulder.

"Lily?" Tommy yelled.

"Are you okay?" Herb shouted.

She smiled. "Tell him that'll be entirely up to you."

"What do you mean?"

"If you do what I want we should have no problems. If you don't . . ." She bared her fangs. "Then we might have some issues."

More pounding. "Devin?" Tommy said. "Open it!"

I turned slightly to face the door.

"Uh-uh!" She wagged her finger. "Don't make a move for that door. I like you, Devin, but I promise that I'll kill you in a heartbeat if I need to."

"Why are you doing all this? Wait a second, how are you still a vampire, even? Your father was killed. Shouldn't that release you from his spell?"

She laughed. "Devin, my father didn't turn me. I turned him."

Her words hammered into me. "What?"

She floated down to the floor. "Oh, yeah. That whole story I told you? Pretty much just reverse it. I was the one bitten. I was turned. I went into the coma. When I woke up, I had this hunger." Her upper lip curled up, highlighting her fang. "My mom didn't stand a chance."

My jaw dropped. "You mean . . . ?"

"It's been so long, I barely even remember her. But my dad. Well, he's another story. A genuinely good guy. He stayed with me through my transition from mortal to vampire, and then when he was worried that I'd stay twelve forever and not have a parent? Well, he allowed me to turn him so he could be with me."

I stared at her. "I'm sorry, Lily."

She took a step toward me. "Don't be."

I instinctively took a step back.

"Some of the stuff that I told you before was true," she said. "We really were hunted by villagers when they discovered we were vampires. Sometimes we barely even made it out alive. But that never deterred my dad. In the back of his mind, he always thought if only mortals got to know us it'd be different. Year after year, town after town, he opened a stupid theater school, figuring creative and artistic people are more accepting. That if only they got to know us, things would be different." She laughed. "But you know what, Devin?"

I shook my head.

"Humans are the same wherever you go," she said. "They're judgmental, opinionated, and suspicious."

"That's awful. I'm sorry that happened to you.

But you can't do this your whole life. You can't keep running."

"Maybe one day." She shrugged. "But right now I'd have to think that when all the bodies are found out in the woods there might be more than a few people angry."

"But that wasn't you. It was Bryce and Delia."

She started laughing. "Devin, you're so gullible. *There is no Delia!*"

Everything started rushing to me at once. Replaying of everything.

"What?" I said. "But I saw her."

Lily reached out, and a wig floated to her. A dark wig with red streaks. She tapped her chest. "I'm Delia. That's why you never saw her face. She's a character I play. When you were with me, I got other girls to wear her wig. When I was a kid and did things to get in trouble, I blamed Delia. My dad always knew when she was mentioned that I was up to something. He even suspected it with you. He was worried about me, but I was still his daughter, so he never stopped me. That was first among the many mistakes he made."

I just stared at her for a moment, seeing her differently. She'd played me. This whole time, she'd played me. "Why?" I muttered.

"I told you the truth in some things, Devin. My dad was really trying to live nicely among the humans.

He wanted us to fit in. To belong. To stop running. But he was naïve. Humans are and will always be bad. There were quite a few of us who disagreed with him. Especially since humans are also . . ." her eyes narrowed . . . "delicious."

I gulped and took another step back. "Please, don't." I whispered.

"Oh, don't worry, Devin. If I had wanted to kill you, I could have done it a thousand times over already. I didn't want to. Though I can't say the same about your idiot cousin and the warlock. I didn't touch them because I didn't want to alert anyone, and you were the perfect candidate to help me do what I wanted."

"What are you talking about?"

"I needed you. I knew you were the perfect one to help me get what I wanted. When I heard about how you saved the town from evil stuffed animals, I knew that you were the perfect choice to face mystical adversaries. You did me a favor."

I had a very bad idea of what she was talking about. "Meaning?"

"You did what I wanted you to do for me. It was pretty easy to make you like me. A simple spell, really."

"I didn't like you on my own? You messed with my mind?" I felt my heart sink.

She stuck out her bottom lip. "You look so hurt. I almost feel bad." She shrugged. "You did like me. But through my powers, I could amplify it by a thousand. Then it was easy to get you to do what I wanted. You got rid of my father for me. Do you know how long I've wanted to do that but never could? I could never bring myself to do it. For sentimental reasons, first of all, but also for appearances. I couldn't lead his clan of vampires if they thought I'd been responsible for killing my own father." She smiled again. "That's where you came in."

I kept taking little steps until my back was pressed against the door. My hands were behind me, and I grasped the door handle.

Still no give.

"But I didn't kill him," I said. "Mr. Flopsy-Ears did."

"Oh, I know that. But they all think you did. Well, whoever's left, anyway. And now they'll blame you—a human—for it, and we can go back to what we do best. Being vampires. That means no more trying to be nice to humans." Her upper lip curled. "We do what we want."

More pounding.

"Devin, open up!" Tommy yelled.

I turned so the side of my face was against the door. "There's a key downstairs in the kitchen drawer!"

Lily took another step. "A key won't open that door. Nor will the warlock's magic." She reached a couple of feet in front of me. "Now, we have a few options, because I need to show the remaining clan something to sink their teeth into, so to speak. I need to either come back with you and your family as vampires in our clan, or as our slaves, or . . . as their dinner." She reached up.

I flinched.

She paused, then touched my face with her nail and dragged it down my cheek. "So, Devin. What's it going to be?" She bared her fangs. "Do you want to be my forever friend?" She leaned closer, until she was just inches from my face. "I promise I'll make it quick. As painless as possible." She looked into my eyes. "And just think, you'll live forever." She took another step. Opened her mouth wide. Her fangs glistened. "Get ready for immortality."

I unfurled my fist and rammed the cross into her forehead.

Her eyes widened and teared. Her forehead sizzled, and a trail of smoke wafted up into the air. She screamed, swatting the cross out of my hand.

It went flying across the room, where it landed somewhere in the dark.

"No!" I yelled, and shoved her out of the way.

I ran straight for the chair by my desk, picked it up, and reared my arm back, ready to throw it through the window and let some sunlight in.

Before I could do it Lily was on me, snatching my arm.

I turned to see a pink-scarred cross seared into her forehead.

She growled. "You're trying to let sunlight in against me?" She yanked the chair out of my hand, lifted me above her head, and threw me against the wall.

I crashed, knocking a mirror off, and fell to the ground, sending shards of glass scattering. "Oof!" I grunted as the air left my body. All I felt was pain. It hurt to breathe. It felt like something was broken.

"Devin!" Tommy's voice from outside. "The key won't open it! It doesn't fit the lock."

Lily jumped at me.

I grabbed one of the shards and swiped it at her, slashing her arm.

She shrieked.

Black blood splattered my hand.

"OW!" I screamed.

The drops felt like acid on my skin. I rubbed my arm against the carpet, trying to wipe it off.

It was that slight distraction, which was all she needed. Suddenly, she was on me. She sank her fangs into my shoulder.

I opened my mouth to scream, but nothing came out. Everything became hazy. The room spun. Swirling mists of dark colors.

I squeezed the broken mirror shard until it cut into my hand.

The warm, wet sensation of my blood trickled down my wrist.

I ignored the pain and brought the shard down into her chest.

Lily let out a shriek like I've never heard. Like a thousand wounded animals dying at once.

Her body morphed before my eyes, from regular Lily, to vampire, and back again. She grabbed my wrist and held it.

Her growl was low. Guttural. "You missed my heart." She backhanded my face, sending me back into the side of my bed. She jumped to her feet. "You no longer have a choice. You're dead."

She was on me fast, slashing at my face.

I held my hands up to block her, but it felt like she was cutting my wrists to shreds.

I kicked her stomach to shove her away and staggered to my feet.

Again, I tried to get to the window, but she slashed at my legs, bringing me to my knees.

I searched the ground for another shard of broken glass from the mirror, but the dizziness started to get to me.

Sweat streamed down my forehead, stinging my eyes. The room was spinning. Whatever she had done to me was starting to take effect.

I found another shard and swung again, but there was no force behind it.

Lily grabbed my arm and chomped down.

Nausea filled me, and I screamed.

I wobbled back and forth, swinging the shard wildly.

"That's two bites, Devin." Lily laughed. "One more, and you're no longer mortal."

I held the shard up.

She got to her feet and stepped back. "You look pathetic. The vampire toxin is taking control of your body. It's only a matter of time." Her eyes twinkled. "I'll tell you what," she said. "Let's play a game." She lifted her arms, and the smoky mist filled the room. The smoke swirled around me. "I won't even tell you what direction it's going to come from so you can be surprised." She disappeared into the swirls of smoke. "Will it be from here?"

I heard her voice to my left, and slashed at the air.

"Or maybe from here?"

I swiped in the other direction.

More laughter.

I scooted back against my night table and banged into it.

Something rattled.

I felt along the top and wrapped my hand around a bottle.

I grabbed it and brought it in front of my face.

One of the bottles of Fresh Florida Sunshine that Herb brought. I laughed to myself. I had absolutely nothing to lose. I smashed the neck part against the night table and held the opened bottle out.

A large yellow beam shot out into the room, lighting everything up.

Lily fell out of the cloud of smoke with a scream, and onto the floor.

She whirled to face me. For the first time, she looked shaken. "What was that?" She was breathing heavily. Her nostrils flared.

She lunged at me.

I grabbed another bottle and smashed it open. Another ray of light. It reflected off of the shards of glass, sending beams of light crisscrossing across the room.

Lily recoiled. Her face started blistering. Little pockets of bubbles popped up all over her skin. She writhed on the floor.

I grabbed another.

She hissed. "You're going to die!"

I shook my head. "No, Lily. You are." I smashed it open, bathing her in a pool of light.

Lily started to tremble and shake violently. She reached out for me.

I backed as far away as I could, pushing the night table nearly into the wall.

She screamed once more. Her face began melting away. Her eyes were the last thing left, melted into a puddle on the floor.

I jumped away from the puddle before it could touch

me, and took a moment to catch my breath. Everything hurt. Blood still streamed down my arm.

I collapsed against my bed.

More pounding on the door.

"Devin?" Tommy called.

"I'm okay. Lily's dead."

"Really?" Herb asked.

I nodded, and realized how stupid that was since nobody could see me. "Really."

"How?" Tommy yelled.

I hated having to tell him. "The bottles of Florida sunshine that Herb bought."

Another pounding on the door. "Yes!" Tommy yelled. "I knew that stuff would work!"

"So open the door," Herb said.

I started to get up. "I'm coming."

Every muscle in my body groaned.

Something whistled.

I looked up. Staring back at me, hanging from the ceiling, was Mr. Flopsy-Ears. And he was holding one of the broken bottles. "Oh, cra—"

He leaped.

CHAPTER THIRTY

YOU CAN'T KEEP A GOOD LAGOMORPH DOWN

I jumped out of the way just as he landed on my bed.

The jagged edge of the bottle shredded my blanket.

I went for the door, but I slipped in the puddle of vampire goo on the floor and went crashing down. My foot felt hot.

Acid!

I stopped to rip my shoe off before it could burn through and onto my foot, but that gave Mr. Flopsy-Ears the advantage he needed. In seconds, he was on me.

He swiped at my face, but I blocked it, placing another gash in my already cut-up arms.

I swatted him off, and he rolled under my bed.

I staggered to my feet and raced for the door. Three feet away, sharp pain slashed at my ankle.

"OW!" I tumbled back down.

"What's going on in there?" Herb yelled. "Open the door!"

"I can't," I said. "I'm being attacked! I told you to get the key."

"Attacked?" Tommy said. "I thought you killed her?"

"It's not Lily!" I shouted back. "It's Mr. Flopsy-Ears!"

"*Mr. Flopsy-Ears?*" they yelled simultaneously.

I lunged for the door handle and twisted.

Still locked.

I banged on the door. "Get the key!"

"We can't find the key!" Tommy said.

I panicked, my heart racing. I turned around and scanned the room.

There were way too many dark, shadowy areas where he could hide.

I pressed my back to the door, so at least he couldn't attack me from behind. "I'm warning you, Mr. Flopsy-Ears. They're going to get the key and open that door any minute. If I were you I'd leave right now."

There was a jingling sound.

Out of the corner of my eye, I saw Mr. Flopsy-Ears standing on my dresser.

He was smiling and twirling a key ring around his paw.

The key to my room was on it.

I pointed at him. "Give that to me!"

He flung the bottle remnant at my head.

I ducked, but it smashed against the door above me and shattered.

Little glass shards, like a mini waterfall, showered down on top of me.

He grabbed another half-bottle and did the same thing. More glass pieces. I could feel them in my hair, down my shirt, sticking to my clothes.

He bent his knees and pushed off from the dresser, launching himself at me.

I ducked, but he managed to grab my hair as he passed overhead. It felt like the strands were about to be yanked out. I threw myself back, squashing him between me and the wall. His grip loosened a little, and I did it again.

Squash.

He grunted.

"You like that, Mr. Flopsy-Ears?" I yelled. "Good, because you're going to get it again!"

Once more, I hurled myself back.

This time he let go and dropped to the floor.

I ran and leaped for the spot where the mirror had broken and picked up a triangle of glass.

I whirled around just as he neared and swiped the shard of glass into him.

He squealed in pain and grabbed his stomach. There was a long gash where his stitches had been.

White cotton fluff, like guts, spilled out between his paws. He tried to shove it back in.

Something inside me snapped.

I'd had enough of being attacked by bloodsucking vampires and murderous stuffed animals.

I screamed and charged. "I HATE YOU, MR. FLOPSY-EARS!"

His eyes widened.

He leaped into the air and rabbit-stomped my face, knocking me back. He jumped on top of me, balling his paws into fists. The punches were fast and furious. He used his ears like flippers to smack my face.

My head started to spin.

The loss of blood and my wounds from both him and Lily were starting to take their toll. Unless I did something fast, Mr. Flopsy-Ears was going to finish me off.

I reached back and plunged the shard into Mr. Flopsy-Ears's chest.

All the punches stopped.

He grabbed my wrist.

I brought the shard down, cutting toward his already opened wound.

Mr. Flopsy-Ears turned to hop away, but I grabbed his tail.

"No, you don't," I said. "You're staying right here!!"

I rolled on top of him, grabbed his throat, and squeezed.

He continued punching me, but I didn't let go.

A couple of feet away, I noticed the gloop-like puddle of Lily's blood.

I pushed him toward it. Mr. Flopsy-Ears continued punching me. It hurt, but I kept going.

Five inches away.

Four.

Three.

Finally, I got him close enough so that his ear grazed the oil-like puddle. With one last burst of strength, I shoved him forward. His ear sank into the puddle and started to sizzle.

Mr. Flopsy-Ears let loose a shriek, higher than any I had ever heard in my life.

Too late, I realized that I'd been so busy staring that I'd released my hold on him.

He snarled and stomped my face.

I let go of his throat, and he chomped down on my wrist.

"Ow!" I yelled.

That brief moment was all he needed. Mr. Flopsy-Ears kicked into my ribs.

I grabbed my side and curled into a ball on the floor.

Already, I could see that part of his ear had disintegrated where it had touched the acid blood.

Mr. Flopsy-Ears bared his teeth. He glanced between me and the window several times before staring down at his chest and stomach. Another piece of fluff fell from the tear.

Mr. Flopsy-Ears pointed at me, then slid his paw across his throat. He grabbed my chair and heaved it through the window. Glass shattered outward, and sunlight filled the room.

Mr. Flopsy-Ears turned to me once more and waved.

I reached out. "Noooo!"

More pounding on the door.

"Devin!" It was Mom's voice.

I heard the key in the lock.

Mr. Flopsy-Ears clutched his fabric together and bounded out the window.

I tried to get up, but the pain in my ribs caused me to crumple to the floor.

The room started to spin.

Everything faded.

Darkness.

CHAPTER THIRTY-ONE

REST, RELAXATION, AND RECUPERATION

The night air hit my face as I soared above the houses of Gravesend. The stars were all out and it was clear. Only a cloud or two in sight. I had never felt so free, so alive.

I spread my arms, closed my eyes, and flew back to my house. I've been doing it for so long, it becomes instinct. You literally can do it with your eyes closed.

My window was open, and I drifted right in. Being a vampire has been an adjustment but after the first hundred years or so, it becomes second nature.

My coffin was open and waiting for me.

I crawled in and pulled the lid closed. It was almost morning, and daylight would be appearing soon. It was all right. I was exhausted. It had been a terrible night of hunting. Not many humans out, so I had to resort to squirrel blood. Squirrels leave such a nasty aftertaste.

I closed my eyes, ready for sleep.

Suddenly, I heard a creaking sound. My eyes popped open. The coffin lid ripped away.

In front of me, with a mallet and wooden stake, was Abby.

She sneered at me. "I told you that I would get you, Devin! No matter how long it took!" She held the stake to my chest and smiled. "Goodbye, Devin!"

She struck the mallet.

I screamed.

"Devin!" A voice snapped me awake.

I looked up and Mom was sitting on the edge of my bed. Actually, it wasn't my bed at all. "Mom, where am I?"

Tommy and Herb suddenly appeared by her side.

Tommy smiled. "Dev! You're okay!"

"You are a resilient lad, Devin," Herb said. "I swear you have more lives than Dobie Gillis has loves!"

"What?" I asked.

Mom pushed the hair away from my eyes and smiled. "Never mind that. You're in Gravesend General."

"The hospital?" I muttered, and for the first time noticed the tubes sticking out of my arms.

She nodded. "Yes, but you're going to be all right. You lost a lot of blood." She dabbed at a tear in her eye. "I was so worried about you. We all were."

I looked around the room and saw Dad asleep in a chair, Abby next to him.

Abby saw me and ran to my side. "Devin!"

"Abby, you're okay!" I said.

She smiled. "You saved me, Devin." She stopped a moment, and looked down. "Thank you."

I smiled back. "I'm glad you're okay."

She reached out and hugged me.

Mom shook her head. "I couldn't believe it. Vampires, in this day and age."

"You heard about everything?" I asked.

"Yes, Tommy and Herb filled me in on all the details." She looked down. "Devin, I'm so sorry that I pushed you to go to the dance with them. She looked so sweet."

"Don't blame yourself, Aunt Megan," Tommy said. "Vampires are sneaky."

"And plus," Herb said, "she was a trained thespian. Those two things alone made it child's play for her."

Tommy nodded. "That's why you always have to live by one rule: *never* trust a vampire."

"Well, I think you're right, Tommy," Mom said. "And to think I let her into our home."

"That's how she managed to get in all those times," Herb said.

"Well, that and Mr. Flopsy-Ears," Tommy said.

"*You saw Mr. Flopsy-Ears?*" Abby shrieked. "Where is he?"

I looked at Abby. "That stupid bunny almost killed me!"

She shook her head. "Mr. Flopsy-Ears wouldn't hurt anyone."

I frowned. "Did you see what he did to me?"

"He was probably scared," Abby said. "He knows you don't like him."

"Everyone stop!" Mom said.

Dad jumped up from his sleep. "I didn't do it!" He looked around. "Oh." He smiled at me, walked over, and tousled my hair. "How are you, Dev?"

"I've been better, Dad, but I'm okay."

Dad put his hand on my shoulder. "From now on, only dances with fully live people, okay?"

I nodded. "I agree."

Abby nudged Dad. "Dad, give Devin the thing."

"Huh?" Dad said. "Oh, yeah!" He reached into his pocket, fished something out, and offered it to me.

It was a necklace with a charm attached that read #1 BROTHER.

I took it from him and smiled. "Thanks, Dad."

"I picked it out!" Abby said.

I laughed. "Thanks, Abby."

Dad put his hand on Abby's back. "Come on, let's give Devin some space."

Abby hugged me again. "Devin, you really are a great brother."

I hugged her back.

Dad and Abby walked to the chairs at the other end of the room and sat.

Herb watched them for a moment, slid his glasses up the bridge of his nose, and leaned down. "You'll be pleased to know that I'm working on a spell that will keep Mr. Flopsy-Ears away. It'll work on any stuffed animals. From what I can deduce, he tried to facilitate your murder at the hands of the vampires since their interests matched his own. He was more than willing to stay hidden until he saw that they were defeated. Then he had to take matters into his own hands. Er, paws."

I fell back in the bed. "So now I have a psycho stuffed bunny after me for the rest of my life?"

"Unless you managed to kill him," Herb said. "We found an awful lot of stuffing outside your window and on the ground outside."

"Nah." Tommy shook his head. "You didn't kill him. He's alive somewhere, plotting his revenge."

"Thanks, Tommy." I sank further back into the pillow.

"But so what?" Tommy said. "The three of us have each other's backs. Nobody's going to beat us!"

Herb thrust his finger into the air. "I concur! We're a modern-day Athos, Porthos, and Aramis!"

Tommy glanced at me. We both shrugged.

Mom stood up. "We can talk about all of this later.

Right now, I think Devin needs some rest." She leaned down and kissed my forehead.

I closed my eyes for a moment. It felt good to do that. "I'm okay, Mom. I'd actually like the company. I'm just happy that everyone's all right."

She smiled back at me. "And we're happy that you are."

"Before we go," Tommy said. "I wanted to tell you that you were amazing. You took on vampires and Mr. Flopsy-Ears all by yourself. I don't know if I could've done that."

"No," I said. "It wasn't by myself. You guys helped me. This was a team effort. You knew everything and told me." I turned to Herb. "And I have to admit your bottled sunshine is what did it."

Herb puffed out his chest. "I knew that gift would come in handy."

I nodded. "It saved my life."

Tommy's expression turned serious. "We need to buy more!"

"Why?" I asked.

"It's Gravesend. You need to take—"

"Precautions." I finished the sentence for him.

I thought about all the pain that I was in, and how lucky that I was able to still be here. I smiled at them. "How about for a few minutes we don't talk about witches, vampires, or killer stuffed animals? And hopefully we don't see any of them again for a very long time."

Mom nodded. "I agree, Devin. And you have my word that the last thing I want is for you to even think about supernatural things. I just want you to rest and take your mind off of this. As a matter of fact, I'm going to make sure that the next thing you do is free of any supernatural event whatsoever."

I smiled. "Yes! Now *that* is something I like to hear."

Herb sighed. "I wish resting like that was a luxury that I had."

I looked up at him. "What are you talking about?"

Herb paused a moment. "Well, normally I don't like to burden friends with my problems, but lately I've been having these really strange dreams."

Mom asked, "Like what?"

Herb's brow furrowed. "It's difficult to explain, but every night my dreams turn dark. Scary. It's almost like someone's been invading my mind and turning them into nightmares. I wouldn't think anything of it, except that it's been happening so frequently." He shrugged. "I'm sure it's nothing, but it's definitely been causing more than one sleepless night. Right now, even an hour uninterrupted would make me feel like Rip Van Winkle."

Tommy's eyes widened. "You know, it could be that you've been attacked by a dream manipulator."

I shook my head. "No! No dream demons! No anything."

Tommy thrust his finger into the air. "I need to research this."

Mom waved her hand dismissively. "There are no such things as dream manipulators. Sometimes a nightmare is just that. There doesn't have to be a reason behind it." She stroked my cheek. "Now, you get some rest and don't worry about a thing."

I fell back into my pillow and groaned. "Yeah, Mom. Because nothing weird ever happens in Gravesend."

THE END

ACKNOWLEDGMENTS

Welcome to Acknowledgments: The Sequel!

Last year, when I wrote my acknowledgments for *Night of the Living Cuddle Bunnies*, I was basically in a daze. It still doesn't feel real, but I'm grateful that I'm getting the opportunity to do it again. So, without further ado, here we go:

There are so many people who had a hand in making this book that my fear is leaving someone out. If I do, please remember that it's not intentional. Again, except for Lester Sherman, whom I refuse to mention, since he had absolutely nothing to do with the making of this book.

With that being said, let's get to the rest.

Each day that I'm in this business, I grow more and more thankful that I have someone like Nicole Resciniti in my corner. Besides being my agent extraordinaire, you have been a great friend and sounding board. When you steer me in a direction, I always know that you have only my best interests at heart. I can't even begin to imagine doing this without you. And no matter how far I go in this business, I'll never forget our deal to clean your house every other week. It's well worth it. No matter how many times I say it, it's still not enough. Thank you.

Toward the end of my first book at Sky Pony, *Night of the Living Cuddle Bunnies*, Kat Enright took over as my editor after two others had left. I was scared and nervous and didn't know what to expect, but you came in and were already familiar with it, and that eased my fears. This time, I got to work with you right from the start, and I couldn't ask for better. Always full of enthusiasm for the Devin Dexter world, your ideas and guidance have truly helped turn *From Sunset till Sunrise* into a much better book than what we started with.

And while we're on the subject, thank you to everyone else at Sky Pony who has continued to support the adventures of Devin Dexter and helped make more of his stories a reality. I love writing them, and am happy that you gave him a home.

There is no way that I'm here without Joyce Sweeney. I wrote last time how Joyce has been an incredible mentor and friend. That's still the case. You're always there for me to discuss ideas with, and to offer sage advice. And I know last time you caught some flak for me writing and telling the world that I was your favorite mentee, so don't worry. I won't mention it again.

Next is my critique group, The Tuesdays. Every week, you hear my stories and always offer the best advice to make it better. We all have our roles in the group, and even though I'm known as the "sensitive one," I think I did a much better job with this book about keeping it together when you critiqued me. So to Joanne Loveday Butcher, Cathy Castelli, Faran Fagen, Melody Maysonet, and Stacie Ramey, I thank you.

Stacie, besides our group, you've also been a great friend. I love that we're always able to turn to each other for support and to discuss writing. And even though it's sometimes awkward when you ask if I think Joyce likes you as much as me, and I have to still answer "no," I think we've never let it get in the way of our friendship.

To everyone in SCBWI Florida, thank you for your kindness. It really is amazing to have such a close-knit group of writers who pull for and support each other. Linda Rodriguez Bernfeld, Dorian Cirrone and the rest of the team, truly do a lot for this chapter, and it shows by how much the people care about each other. There are way too many people to mention individually, but when you go to a conference here, it feels like everyone is your friend, and that's a great feeling to have.

In these days of being able to communicate virtually with each other, there are other writers I've been fortunate enough to connect with, who I'm now even more fortunate enough to be able to call friends. Wendy McLeod MacKnight and Melissa Roske, I love our chats on social media and the support given to each other.

Melissa, thank you for still being there to commiserate with and offer encouragement to each other.

I'm also lucky enough to call Lee Wardlaw a friend. Lee is a fantastic author and guardian angel. Thank you for your friendship and advice. It's always valued and appreciated.

Now on to my non-writing life. Last book, Paul Kallwitz promised me twenty dollars to put him in the acknowledgements. Well, he still hasn't paid. If anyone sees him, please call him out on it.

Again, I've received many messages asking if my favorite part of this book is different than the last. Well, if you must know, I still gave extra attention to page twenty-four, but this time it was extremely difficult. Check back on the next book and see if you can guess what page my favorite is then!

To Mom, who just loves hearing every little detail about my writing endeavors. I told her that in the writing world, it's Stephen King, J. K. Rowling, and me. Please don't anyone tell her differently.

To my sister Suzanne, the Snyder family, and everyone in the Wexler family, thank you for your support. But really, you need to ask yourselves, can you do better? So hurry up and start working the book for me. To nephews and niece, Avi, Eitan, Oren, Eidan, Spencer, and Brynn, what's the deal? You should be out there every single day on social media and to your friends, working it. What's more important: an education, or selling books for Tio? Don't answer, it's rhetorical. Unless I see better efforts, you can be sure your reviews won't be so great at our next quarterly family meeting.

Perhaps my most important acknowledgement is to the readers, teachers, librarians, parents, grandparents, and any caregiver who rallied behind *Night of the Living Cuddle Bunnies*. I can't even begin to express the thrill I got when I saw good reviews or messages come in from actual readers, and even better were the ones from kids. When you write, you hope it finds an audience, and you hope people enjoy it. Every time someone talks to me about a scene they loved, or who their favorite character is, it gives me such a great feeling of overwhelming happiness. I thank each and every one of you. You're who I do this for, and I hope you continue to enjoy the adventures of Devin, Tommy, Abby, Herb, and the rest of the Dexters. I'll write them as long as you enjoy reading them.